THIS LONELY
CARCASS SONG

A COLLECTION OF HORRORS
NICK HARPER

CONTENTS

THE RAGE

He moaned, grit tumbling out of his eyes as they snapped open. Clutching at ribs that burned like they'd been snapped, his head lolled forward and he looked down. His knees were blotchy and bruised, wafer-thin skin pulled tight over bony joints; the ground beneath them was a flat, silver-flecked vinyl. Hospital blue, shining and smeared as if someone had polished it recently.

The man jolted suddenly, neck straightening as he realised he was knelt on the floor. He tried to move, or to stand, but his arm was bent up behind his head. He drew in a sharp, shallow intake of breath as pain curled around the muscles in his back. His elbow was coiled around the nape of his neck and his fingers were curled like bony hooks around the plastic bars at the foot of some bed he couldn't remember falling out of. His head tipped back, numb and heavy with a dull aching sensation – frayed nerves, bridging the gap between spine and brain stem, crackled with the bitter remnant of some recent agony – and the man blinked up into fluorescent strips of light that flickered and crackled in a gridlock ceiling.

He couldn't remember his name.

'Where am I?' he murmured, speech slurred enough that all three words seemed to melt into one incomprehensible mess of sound. His tongue was heavy and there was a warmth in his cheek where blood had swelled around his aching teeth. It drizzled from one nostril, too, and with his free hand he swiped at the beads of red on his top lip, wiping his mouth with a gaunt wrist. The room seemed familiar, but any memory of it was trapped, just out of reach: visible through the haze of a barbed-wire mesh in his mind but farther away the closer he moved to it.

The man blinked, turning his head to look around. His neck cracked with the movement and he winced, teeth gritted in gums that felt shredded and thin. The tendons in his shoulders stung, stretched to the point where they felt as though they could snap. His whole body hurt, craned into a position so uncomfortable he wondered how he had managed to wind himself there: his knees were bent back beneath his rump, legs splayed, wiry with hair, and poking out of the hem of a pastel-green gown; his feet were bare and purple-stained toes curled upward off the floor, blistered ankles straining. His soles were slick with blood but there were no wounds or scars there; the blood belonged to someone else. The man's back arched and as he tried to straighten it something popped loudly at his hip. He cried out, throat stringy and hoarse.

'Hello!' he croaked. He thought about calling for a nurse, or an orderly, but he didn't know if he was in a hospital or if this was all some crooked dream. It felt real, hard and solid and cold, and he had never had a dream like this. Not that he could remember...

He clutched at his ribs, suddenly, as the pain that lined the edges of his chest spread to the very middle and jabbed narrow blades into the mucus-coated walls of his lungs. His hand came away wet and warm and red and his eyes dropped to the gown; blood was splashed across it in a jagged spatter, like some monstrous thing had tapped the head of a metre-long brush and sprayed him with paint. His breathing quickened and he wiped his palm frantically along the folds of the gown, only succeeding in staining it further until the only thing he could do was slap it against the surface of the floor and smear the blood in curls and spirals over the vinyl. He screwed his eyes shut, panicking, in an attempt to control himself but all he could think (*where am I*) was that he remembered nothing about this room, remembered nothing about *coming* here (*where am I*) or being brought here, or *dragged* here (*who am I*) and the only thing he knew at all was that he was here, now, and that he ached.

His eyes opened again and he looked.

The room was long and narrow – maybe about thirty

7

feet by fifteen, although his head was pounding so hard and his depth perception so muted that he fancied it might have been anywhere between thirty and ninety, between fifteen and forty-five, and why did it matter?

'Focus,' he murmured, clapping his blood hand against his temple. His breathing threatened to quicken again and he paused, drawing it in slowly, letting it out slower still. *Relax,* he thought. Focus on the *where*. The *who* can come later.

Either side of the room, a row of plastic-framed beds was arranged so that ugly, plastic headboards were pressed to the padded, white walls and there was a two-foot gap between each. It almost reminded him of a summer-camp dormitory, except for the sterile colours and the smell: clinical and flowery, bleach and rosewater. Beside each bed was a low, wooden cabinet with rounded, white-plastic covers tacked to every corner; some seemed to be filled with papers and books, others packed with wiring and crowned with blinking monitor screens. He could hear a faint, rhythmic beeping in the background, not the ticking of a clock but the

blip

of a heart-rate monitor. He looked for it, but there was none in the room, and indeed it sounded

blip

like it was coming from beyond the walls. So it was a hospital ward, then, and he was in a hospital. That must be why he couldn't remember anything, and where all the blood had come from – there had been an accident, or something, and that was of course a perfectly reasonable explanation except (*there's no one else here*) for the fact that he was entirely alone in the room, and on the floor.

Above his head, the fluorescent lights buzzed faintly. A strange warmth drifted down onto him from the glass-encased bulbs but it was almost pleasant; the room was cold, and not the kind of cold that came with a controlled air-conditioning system or a fan, but the kind one might feel walking through a cemetery very early in the morning. He shivered a little.

There were no windows on the ward; the only light came from the sizzling bulbs overhead and through a glass slit in a black door at the far end of the room. He looked for a while at the door, watching for shapes through the glass, but there was no movement – none that he could see from here, anyway. The smell lingered in his nostrils, disinfectant and crushed flowers and copper, and his head had cleared a little. The room made some sense to him now. To his left, the empty beds were spread evenly all the way to the door, wheels at their feet hammered down with rusted brakes. The vinyl floor was bathed in blue.

To his right, a bulb had died and the beds were no more than long, rectangular shapes swallowed by shadows. Shades moved in the dark. The man watched as writhing silhouettes twisted, grey and crisp at the edges of the room, soundless and without faces or features.

'Hello?' he called. 'Hello, can anybody tell me where I...'

He trailed off. There was no sound, other than the low, electric hum of the light closest to him and a slow, shallow breathing that he felt must be his own. But there was a presence, somewhere in the room, a pulsing heat and a heartbeat so thick and heavy that he fancied he could feel it along with his own; two strings of thudding rhythm threaded about each other, out of sync but somehow melodic. Hardly thinking, he squinted into the shadows.

There was a shape in one of the beds, at the far end of the room. He could barely make it out in the dark but it watched him, draped in darkness and completely still, a mound of nothing rising up from the sagging mattress in a drifting haze of half-formed silhouettes. Grey static sparkled at the edges of the man's vision and he blinked.

'Hello,' he addressed the shape. He swallowed. 'Can you hear me? I... where am I?'

He tried to stand, but something pulled at his wrist. He frowned, tilting his head back, yanking at the thing to try and free his hand. It was cold and tight and it dug a little into his flesh, pinning his arm to the foot of the bed. He twisted, straining to see, and with the movement his foot shot out from beneath him and his toes collided with something sharp and cool on the floor.

Distracted, the man turned his head, following the direction of his narrow leg, sinuous and malnourished (he had vague memories of his own shape, his own form, and he was quite sure he had never been as thin and decayed as this; perhaps he had been in this room for longer than he could think to remember), and saw that a clipboard had fallen from a hook on the bed across from him. A plastic clipboard, with a sheet of handwritten notes pinned to it.

Grunting as he stretched out his leg, he pawed at the clipboard with his foot. Pain shot through his arm, through his whole left side, and he grimaced. Tangled black hair had fallen in his eyes, curled and matted with sweat and gritty enough that, when he raised his free hand to push it back, silt filtered through his fingers. His ankle pinned the board to the vinyl floor and he retracted his leg, pulling it close enough to grab.

He read slowly, lips moving to the shape of every scrawled word, eyes squinting in the half-light. *Patient Notes,* read a heading at the top of the page in neatly-printed script. Black ink spattered the corners of the crinkled page. This confirmed it, he thought: he was in a hospital. Or at least a doctor's facility of some kind. But – he glanced up, checking to make sure he hadn't imagined it – there was a lock on the inside of the door.

He was quite certain there shouldn't be, in a hospital

ward. And there was an air about this place, a quiet, ominous air that told him he was somewhere else entirely. He had vague memories of hands bundling him forward, tripping over the kerb and into the road; there was a van, back doors swinging open, groping fingers digging into his armpits through the material of a ratty, smoke-scarred coat.

He paused, trying to draw in on the image, to remember the faces of the men in the white coats and the driver of the van. He remembered a bench, cold metal beneath his flank, the zip of a cable tie – and then nothing.

Briefly, his eyes turned to the thing at the end of the room, the thing hunched over on the mattress with a sheet of shadows covering its face. He wondered if it was a man, like him, brought here by those same vague fingers in that same, reeking van. He wondered if the figure under the sheet was the "patient". It must be. There was nobody else here. And yet, that smell…

He read on:

Patient 013 responded badly to his first treatment with experimental drug X237-PPR. Something in the mix of deca-durabolin and psilocybin reacted, despite the careful administration, with something quite unseen already in his system, and has resulted in a state of unadulterated fury rather unlike anything we have ever encountered.

The subject has been sedated for now, but the symptoms we witnessed in the few minutes the drug reigned in his system included, all at once: reddening of the corneas; violent spasms of the hands and arms; greatly-increased strength; most significantly, an unrelenting and catastrophic fit of somewhat animalistic rage. The patient's inhibitions seemed removed by the drug, mirroring – but with greater ferocity – some of the side effects that patient 008 exhibited. Loss of some motor functions, lack of emotional control.

The subject has been temporarily restrained. Further tests are required, but until it can be proven the symptoms were a result of the mixing of X237 and some parasitic entity already existing within the subject's body, and not purely that of the drug alone, it must be deemed UNFIT for public distribution. Indeed, in the case at least of this subject, the drug proved only one thing: that a man is capable of expressing hatred and anger in such perfect colour that he might be degraded, downgraded, no longer a man at all, but a monster.

He swallowed. Slowly, he looked back into the shadows. The shape in the bed at the end of the room – The Patient, the man corrupted by this drug and turned to rage and hunger by it – had not moved but it was still staring at him from beneath its veil of mottled, grey shade. Every now and then the shadows moved around the thing's crest, as though it were breathing rapidly and erratically. He could picture it smiling beneath the bedsheet. The clipboard in his hands juddered and he glanced back at the thing, turning the first page over. The second was an image, a black-and-white, printed photograph of a man with his face torn away. Bloody fingerprints caressed the corner of the page. The stump of his neck was a ragged, crumbling mess of savaged white.

The Patient had ripped away his own face.

Silently, hardly daring to breathe himself, the man turned back the page and his eyes darted once again over the doctor's report. He read it again, again, terrified that if he looked up the thing beneath the sheets would know that his attention had shifted and it would come for him. A single word stood out to him from the report and his blood ran cold:

rage

The thing in the shadows made a noise, suddenly,

breath hitching in a coarse, rabid throat.

The man jumped, heart crashing against his cracked ribs. Something at his raised, bent-up wrist rattled loudly, close to his ear. The metallic sound rang out through the length of the ward and he clapped his free hand over his mouth as though that might halt the echo somehow, as if the jangle of chains had come from his own belly.

Cautiously he looked up, toward his lifted hand, and he saw it. It glinted in the electric light, a ring of silver around his wrist with rough, orange-tinted edges that had drawn tiny beads of blood out of his skin. He pulled at his arm and the heel of his palm ground against the metal. Twisting, he winced as the edge of the ring dragged a needle-thin, crimson cut out of his skin.

He was handcuffed to the bars.

'What the…'

The man tugged at a salt-encrusted chain and the cuffs rattled again. Something seemed to move in the shadows and he grimaced, reaching up to twist at the chain with his good hand. He grabbed it, wrapping fingers around metal links that felt old and thin. Flakes of copper dust peeled off of them and drifted over the pads of his fingers, fluttering to the ground.

He was panicking again, suddenly, all thoughts of the shape at the end of the room forgotten and replaced by a thick, hot fear that he had been *left* here for it, that someone had locked him in here with whatever abomination they'd created. He was food – they had taken him off the street and dragged him here to feed the mad, drugged creature, to satiate some animal hunger the experiment had awakened in it.

(*Get out*)

The man twisted his body around and pressed his heel against the bedframe, pushing it back to the wall and arching his back to tug at the handcuffs with both arms. The links seemed weak, almost as if he could (*Christ, why can't I remember my own* fucking *name?*) break them apart easily, but they wouldn't give. 'Come on,' he hissed, tugging and pulling, ignoring the wrenching in his chest and the pain in his shoulder. 'Come on…'

The shadows stirred.

Desperate, the man yanked at the cuffs and grunted, chest pounding (*sedated for now, but*) with terror. The shadows were the pet snake of a sadistic child and he was the poor, white mouse dangled in the cage, fat fingers pinching his tail and swinging him round gleefully, just out of reach of those venom-laced teeth until (*for now*) the kid let go. Except he was bound and gagged, too, stubby legs tied beneath him, stapled by his blood-matted fur to the bars of the cage, and the snake (*rage*) was a python, a boa constrictor injected with heroin and angrier (*dangerous and terrifying*) than it had ever been.

(*GET OUT*)

Suddenly the chains gave way and he was flung backward, tumbling over his own bent-up legs. The gown flitted about him as he rose to his bare feet, shaking, half a handcuff dangling from his bloody wrist. He wiped his hands on the torso of the gown, avoiding the wet patches of blood; he could feel his ribs beneath the material, pressing up so hard and angular (*when did I last eat?*) they could cut through his skin. He looked toward the end of the room and blinked. Shadows writhed around the shape in the bed, the shape of rage buried in a pall of thin, white linen painted grey by the dark.

He turned towards the door and staggered for it, bare feet slapping the vinyl floor with every step. He could see faint silhouettes through the security glass, grey curls that darted past the window and disappeared, long shadows on the pearly slit in the door. They shifted and danced in the orange light of a long corridor and he pressed his face to the window, looking out as far as the edges of his vision would allow.

The corridor walls were painted, splashed crudely with red and white like some finger-art mural in a kids' nursery, drizzled with fleshy pink and shining, glistening-wet purple. He tried the handle: it clattered in his trembling hand and he tugged violently at the door but it wouldn't budge, jammed into the frame. Locked, he thought, remembering the metal knob he'd seen beneath the door handle. He reached down and fumbled with the lock and it ground open – he looked over his shoulder at the linen-draped sheet in the dark and for a moment relief (*escape*) flooded him.

The Patient watched as he tried the door again.

Nothing. The handle jerked and twisted in his grip but the door held fast. He looked, yanking at the handle, pushing and pulling and pressing his forearm to the black wood, and then he realised his mistake and his pounding heart sank into his groin.

The door was locked from outside as well.

He groaned, head falling forward so his brow pressed against the window and the matted, knotted hair in his eyes spread greasy silt on the glass. He could see the shape of the thing through a slit of light at the edge of the doorframe; a thick, iron bolt slid across to shut him in.

'Help me!' he yelled suddenly, shocked at the sound of his own voice. He raised a fist and pounded on the door, bruised fingers aching. The half-chain of the snapped handcuffs clacked against the window. 'Can anyone hear me? Someone get me out of here!'

He looked behind him. The thing still hadn't moved, not an inch. It watched him from its bed, eyeless and silent. Maybe it was still sedated. Maybe it wasn't sitting up at all – just a trick of the crackling, fluorescent light or of his wrecked mind. Maybe they'd drugged him too, that was why he couldn't (*your own* name) remember anything. Maybe they'd (*who are they?*)

drugged them all. All these empty beds couldn't be there for nothing, there had been (*where the fuck are you?*) others.

'Please! Let me out!'

More shapes crashed past the window and he reeled. They were flies, he realised. Tiny little specks of black tumbling over manic, frenzied paths through the air. He could hear them, even from in here, flitting past the door and casting long, tampered shadows on his skin. They buzzed about the corridor, swarming over something long and misshapen on the floor. He looked closer.

Streaks of crimson crashed outward from the shape and he glimpsed an arm, fingers bent and broken, flesh torn away in red, messy strips. The woman's hair was smeared with red and her eyes had been pressed out of her skull, popped in two gelatinous, dark rings in a face frozen in a silent scream.

He turned, pressing his back to the door. Panting. She was dead. He had never seen a dead body before. And there was one three feet from him, just the other side of the door he couldn't unlock, buzzing already with flies and broken and bloody.

(*rage*)

'What are you?' the man breathed.

The thing beneath the sheet didn't respond. He thought it might have moved, just a few inches closer. There was a new weight on the mattress, something that had pressed it over the rim of the bedframe. Maybe it wasn't sedated at all, but waiting.

The man pressed away from the door and into the ward, moving now towards the thing, ploughing forward with something that he would much rather call bravery than (*don't kid* yourself) the other thing. The thing was a man, like him, a person. He could talk to it, reason with it. Maybe the rage hadn't completely overtaken it – it was waiting, after all, patiently. It might respond, if he just spoke to it.

He took careful steps over the vinyl floor, silent except for the shallow breathing that echoed in a hollow, cavernous throat. His hand shuddered at his waist and the severed links of the chain seared his fingers with cold. The aching in his chest had numbed but his skull pounded, hot blood in his ears throbbing so that he could barely hear himself think. Halfway across the room he paused, beneath the last flickering bulb, and watched the thing in the bed.

The sheet folded over its face rose and fell with every shallow breath. Everything was grey, in the depths of the room, but there were dark patches all over the shape that almost shone, as if something slick and black had splashed it.

'Listen to me,' the man said, raising a hand. He frowned, momentarily, noticing the blood crusted beneath his fingernails, dry and flaking. 'Listen. I don't know what you are, or… where we are… I don't know if you can still understand me. But you're still a man, whatever they did to you. You can talk to me, right?'

The thing said nothing.

He took another step and shadows fell over him as he crossed into the dark half of the room. 'Please, listen to me. We're both trapped in here, but we don't have to… we can get out. You and me. If you're still in there, we can…'

I don't even know my own name, he thought. I don't know yours. I don't know if it's daylight outside

(*does that matter?*)

or if the rest of this building is empty save for the carcass in the hallway –

He froze as something cold and wet soaked the pad of his bare foot. He glanced down, saw that he had pressed his toes into the edge of the puddle and thin, black fluid seeped around the spread flesh of his sole. The coppery smell was stronger here, the disinfectant stench left behind and replaced with the scent of death and ruin and butcher's offcuts. Blood crept up through the gaps between his toes and trickled away over the floor.

'Oh my god,' he breathed.

The puddle spread into the dark, touched with highlights of silvery fluorescence at its edges like the wash of a great, black lake; corpses lay sprawled in the mess, spilling off bedframes and knotted around each other.

A dark-skinned, elderly man had tried to hide

beneath one of the beds and the fingers of his left hand were still wrapped around a white, plastic leg. His eyes were wide open and they shone in the dark, glinting like cat's eyes in a blanket of tarmac. His right arm had been torn off at the shoulder and his stump was sinuous and pocked with bite-marks.

The arm was halfway across the room.

The old man's gown was in tatters and the skin of his torso was shredded, not by teeth or the claws of some ravenous monster but by fingers, human fingers strong enough to dig into his flesh as though it were the cool, wet meat of a chicken and rip it outward in a spray of pink and red.

Fearful eyes tracked trails of blood across the floor: a young man lay bent backwards in some spasmic gymnastics pose, chest ruptured and ribs caved inward, heart plucked out and strewn in ribbons across his gut; a red-haired woman had had her legs split open and her cracked pelvis poked through the flesh of her groin in flashes of sheared white.

Another woman lay on her back with her head slumped against the wall. The thing beneath the sheet had gnawed at her throat, torn out a chunk of her with its teeth and yanked her oesophagus forward so the purple, cartilaginous tube looked like a suitcase handle jutting out of her neck. Her belly had been ripped open and coils of intestine spiralled into the shadows, half-visible and still, somehow, twitching, slithery snakeskins wrapped around bulging, bubbling ropes of shit.

He looked at the thing beneath the sheet and shook his head. 'Please,' he whispered. 'Don't hurt me. I can help you. I can get us out of here, if you'll just…'

Hot breath drifted up from where he had imagined the thing's face might be, under the linen mask.

He took a shaky step back and something soft and fleshy burst under his heel. He cried out, pressed his palm to his mouth with such force the snapped handcuff slapped his throat.

The thing in the bed moved, just an inch. It was shivering. Something rose up from its belly, extended from a sheathed hip like a thick, clawed arm reaching for him.

'Please,' the man said, raising his hands. His breathing was laboured and careful. His chest flitted madly. 'Let me just…'

He moved forward, stepping over clumps of indiscernible flesh. There was a spatter of shining, pink brain on the floor to his right. Some of it had splashed the wall above one of the beds and he glanced across, following the wet carnage until he saw a punctured, deflated lung splayed across the pillow. The stench slipped into his throat and he gagged, dry-retching a little.

Reaching the thing's bed, he leant forward a little. The creature smelled of blood and sweat and some bitter, foul thing that had stained it, defiled it. Slowly, the man opened his mouth. 'Listen, if you can still understand me, I'm about to take this sheet off you, okay? Please, don't… I just want to help. Okay?'

The thing beneath the sheet didn't move. It made him uneasy, this close; sitting perfectly still in the middle of the mattress, legs folded so that the folds of the cover poked out around it. Blood-stained linen shivered over its mouth and fell straight down past its hunched shoulders.

He lifted a hand to the corner of the sheet and tugged.

White shadows fell away and the man stumbled back as cloth fluttered around his knees.

'Jesus, what…'

The thing in the bed looked up at him with wide, round eyes, wet with tears and ringed with exhaustion.

'You're not…'

The girl couldn't have been out of her early twenties. She was small, narrow-shouldered with slender arms and legs. Her black hair was pulled back from a pretty face and it stuck up in bloody, curled tufts about her temples. Her cheek was spattered red and her throat was bruised in the pattern of a set of purple, blotchy fingers. She wore the uniform of a student nurse and her legs were folded in pleated, blue trousers. Her left eyelid was pinned down and bruised.

There was a gun in her hand, pointed at him.

Silver glinted in the half-light and her whole arm

shook. 'Please,' she moaned, lifting the gun a little so the tip of the barrel was aimed right at his throat. 'Please, don't hurt me.'

He stumbled back. The blood beneath his nails…

(*rage*)

Slowly, he looked down. His knees were bruised and there was blood on his gown. Pressing, wet and cold, to his chest, so tight that he wondered he hadn't noticed before just how *much* of it there was. Pint-glasses, spilled over his chest and his guts, litres and gallons of red spraying the cloth and spattering the tops of his legs.

He felt something dig at the back of his skull, a tight, crisp pain that clawed at his hair and sent a shiver down his back.

The girl's eyes darted to his hand and he looked down, saw that it had clenched into a tight, red fist. They hadn't (*temporarily* restrained) cuffed him to the bed to feed him to the thing, he was (*The Patient*) the thing. He couldn't remember his name (*Patient*), but he remembered, now, the needle, glistening and fine as it neared his eyeball and (*rage*) slid into the jelly of his cornea. He remembered screaming –

'Please!' the nurse rasped, and he looked down. He realised he was still screeching, not with fear or anguish but with a guttural, animal fury that burned in his chest. His hands were wrapped around the young woman's throat and his thumbs pressed into the soft flesh beneath her ears, digging at the base of her skull. Her eyes were wide and tearful and she croaked, gagging as he pressed his palms into her skin and folded his fingers into the shape of the bruise on her neck.

She raised the gun.

He felt… strong, tight muscles popping and rippling in his neck, his shoulders. He could feel the corners of his mouth pulling upward in a cruel twist of a smile but he couldn't stop it, couldn't turn them down again. His eyes were wild and rabid and his vision was clouded with red. Flashes of (*rage*) violent memories tore across the burning back of his mind as he wrenched the elderly man's arm from his body and flung it across the room, as he leapt on the woman and clamped his teeth down on her throat, ripping and pulling and loving every second of it as the drug in his blood pumped warm and ecstatic and the (*something quite unseen already in his system*) drug turned every emotion to fury and hatred.

Blood splashed his wrists and he blinked, half-expecting to see the young nurse's throat popped open in his hands. The rage filtered away for a moment and he looked down. The gun was pressed to his belly and he smelled cigarette smoke. He stepped back, releasing her neck.

'I…' he gasped. Red foam bubbled over his lips as he looked down.

Through the hole in his gut, he saw flickering, fluorescent lights and strings of meat that hung off his ribs. He crashed to the floor and shockwaves spiralled up his legs from bruised, fractured knees.

In the last second before everything turned black and the wild, bloody spots before his eyes stopped dancing, he remembered his name.

CARRION GODS

Wendy's bare feet bled on the tarmac but she kept walking, raw, peeling soles leaving red tracks in the blistered, sun-cracked earth. It beat down on the back of her neck, puling waves of heat tumbling over her shoulders and making her arms heavy. Bare, dark-skinned legs glistened with sweat beneath the frayed hem of a pair of denim shorts that clung to her thighs and the still folds of a faded hoodie tied around her waist. Beads of salt drizzled down the sides of her face, slick and shining as they brushed the curves of coffee-stain cheeks flaking with exhaustion. Her lips were dry and as cracked as the road beneath her feet, her hair matted to the top of her skull and slipping out of a loose, tangled bun in curls of black and grey.

She breathed with parted lips, tongue dry and plastered to the bottom of her mouth. She wanted to pause, to stop walking altogether, but it compelled her, pulled her forward with all the force of some invisible pair of hands on the lapel of her blouse. She had opened the top three buttons but it was hardly enough to cool her and the sun curled over her chest with a hot, bristled tongue as dry as her own. It felt as though the heat had started to bake the dye out of her hair and it flayed her scalp, imaginary rivers of black ink coursing over her forehead and running down the bridge of her nose. It called her onward with a voice like ice: *Wendy*...

Her knee buckled and her whole body dipped, momentarily, but she stumbled on, walking along the edge of the road like it were a tightrope. It was long, longer than it had ever seemed before, wide enough for two cars to pass each other quite easily, but Wendy had seen nothing for days but the circling buzzards overhead and the flies that crowned rags and strips of roadkill. Either side of the tarmac path brittle wheat stalks rose in swaying, breeze-brushed sheets from earth that seemed too dry and powdery to sustain them. The dirt was bathed in sunlight, orange and rippling like sand, and the fields were burned and blackened.

'How much further?' she moaned, but the voice was, for once, silent. The bottoms of her feet were blistered, shredded by the road and the sharp grains of gravel that drifted over it in the uncomfortable, warm breeze. Her ankles felt half-sprained and a hot, deep ache tore at the ligaments in her legs; her belly was caved, ringed with a cool, hollow pit that had set in as the first hints of starvation had worn at her gut and hadn't eased off since. Her chest was dull and silent, heartbeat slowed so far it was almost non-existent. Christ, she was thirsty. 'Please,' she rasped, 'I've been walking for days… can't I stop? I need to…'

Wendy. Come…

'Please. Please, I just need…'

Come.

She kept walking, glancing over her shoulder with a neck stiff from being held up on her shoulders. Nothing behind her, save for a dark smudge in the middle of the road that hopped and writhed as if it were following her scent, a raven with a beak bloody from dipping into the bellies of tyre-flattened badgers and wings tipped with sharp, brittle feathers. She had seen it a couple of times now, circling the wheat fields and waiting, at the side of the road, for her to pass. She had called it Freddie, on the first day, but all the humour was gone from her now and her thoughts were too dull to remember where the name had come from.

She hadn't slept. The voice hadn't allowed it. *Come,* it said, whenever she slumped at the edge of the path or her head dipped, eyelids heavy and sticking. *Come,* it said, louder. And whenever she ignored it the voice turned to some loud, indescribable whine, a piercing shriek that crashed through her eardrums and burned the back of her skull. When it had first called she had walked blindly, following with light feet, treading carefully over the rough ground on the balls of them so that they would be less easily pricked by the dust and the gravel fragments. Now, though, she walked with clumsy, heavy steps that slapped the tarmac and sent numb little shocks up the length of her shins. It had told her not to wear shoes. *Pain is sacrifice,* it said. *Wendy*...

Behind her, the raven pecked at a slither of blood flecked with dark scraps of dead skin, drinking with a thirsty, grey tongue.

A dull, grey shape at the edge of the road grew clearer as she neared it, and she saw that it was ragged and soaked with blood. The thing could have been a squirrel or a rabbit or a hare but its face was all mangled, clumps of pale, tufted hair pressed against mashed-up ears from a crushed skull spilling with brains. The pressure of the tyre that had squashed down its spine had pushed its tongue out of its mouth in a slip of hideous, neon pink but even that had been flattened and its bone-white snout poked out of a ruff of gritty fur, teeth spread and cracked. A bony hind leg bent out behind its rump and the bones showed through trails of savaged skin in flashes of grey where some death-feeder had picked them clean. The only remnant of the poor creature's insides, the only piece of it that hadn't been chewed-up and swallowed by buzzards and maggots, was a coil of shining grey the size of Wendy's palm that tumbled out of its belly and leaked clear fluid on the tarmac from a shallow slit in its membrane.

Wendy balked and staggered into the middle of the road, walking a wide half-circle past the smeared creature and turning her head. Already the raven had caught up to it and she watched as it hammered its beak into the slick, grey insides of the thing. It seemed content to pick at the leftovers that even the buzzards hadn't fancied and its snout came away wet with mucus as it looked up at her with hungry, shining black eyes.

She kept walking.

Come, the voice told her, and she winced at the sound. It was sorrowful, gruff in its tone but weighted with an edge of heartbreak. She knew it was angry but there was a kindness, somewhere in its words: *Your sacrifice is welcome. Come, Wendy… you draw close.*

'How close?' she breathed, panting in the heat. 'Please, give me a sign or something. I can hear you, I *know* you can hear me. Please… how much farther?'

Come, it said.

'I have a job,' she murmured. 'I work in an office. Listen, they… they'll know I've gone. I didn't call in sick, or… I need a drink. Please.'

The voice fell silent, faded into the heat like the unstable memory of something she had convinced herself she would do better to forget. Her bloody soles smacked the ground as she hobbled on, plagued with thirst and hunger and exhaustion. Her eyelids fluttered. Around her, the burnt wheat-stalks danced in the mocking thrall of a hot, hungry wind. The sky above her head was blood-red and it smelled like bonfire smoke and hamburger grease. She could feel herself salivating but there was no fluid in her mouth, just dust and heat. Her lungs felt brittle and deflated, intestines coiled and tight and wrenching at the strings of her gut.

She collapsed, suddenly, knees knocking the ground as a pang of agony curled against the walls of her womb and squeezed. Her head pounded with sleep-deprived shivers of crashing, rocking pain and her eyes swam behind a mess of purple-tinted spots. *Stand,* said the voice, and she tried, but her legs had given in altogether and she fell forward onto her elbows, grazing them on the tarmac. Her shoulders buckled and her skull smacked the road, eyes closed. The voice turned to a whistle, a torrid electric whine that drove needles into her skin, but she couldn't move, couldn't lift herself out of the dust. Exhaustion, wound around her brain stem from thirty-eight hours on her feet with no rest, no food, won control of her body and she crashed, and unconsciousness swallowed her like a dark, silent beast in the heat from the sun.

Wendy slept, and for a while her thoughts were little more than a loud, shrill carnage of darkness and static. Then the dream came, and it came with no warning, consuming her sleeping mind with all the crashing suddenness of a newly-diagnosed tumour. She had returned to the road, but the ground beneath her knees was not the same rough tarmac as before; now, it was a blanket of thin, dark blood, rippling with the touch of a cold wind's cruel fingers. The wheat had burned all the way down to the roots and the blood swilled over ground-up stems. Husks floated around her like the crushed bodies of a thousand withered locusts.

She heard the roar of a car engine and looked up, turning her face to the sun. It crackled, angry tendrils of white flaring off its surface and lacing the sparse clouds with faint, golden ringlets. It was beautiful, but it made her blood cold. There was no car, just a man, standing ankle-deep in the blood where the end of the road had been. He was far enough away that he should have been no more than a smear of shade on the scarred horizon, but she could see his face as clearly as she might if he were six feet from hers.

He was dressed all in white; white, pleated trousers fluttered softly at the ankles of narrow legs; an ivory blazer was pinned to his torso and a gold chain tumbled across the pockets of a gleaming, white waistcoat. His shirt and tie were pale and his arms hung at his sides, long and slender. His hands were dressed in white, leather gloves that slid softly over bony fingers. His shoes were black, and shining: patent-leather brogues capped at their toes with silver skulls that glinted in the sunlight. But he had no face, and Wendy could not help but stare at the polished mask of bone that he wore atop a narrow, sinuous throat.

He held out a white-gloved hand and she took it, without touching him, rose to her feet in the blood. She was naked, stripped of the shorts and the blouse and the old hoodie that had belonged to her brother until he'd grown out of favour with it. Her skin was dry, and cool, and she felt his hands on her waist, sticky leather caressing her hips. She wanted him to leave her, to turn and walk back to the horizon, but when she looked down his hands were still dangling by his sides. There was, at once, both a mile-wide distance between them and no space at all. She could smell his breath, through cracks in the mask, the breath of a smoker. His exposed wrists were slim and carved with spiralling, throbbing veins and black bristles crowned the bones at the rim of his hands.

'What are you?' Wendy breathed. Her mouth never opened but her voice tore at the air as if she had screamed. 'Why are you doing this to me?'

The man in the white suit and the bone mask tilted his head, just a little, so that his antlers bent and cracked. The mask had been ripped from the picked carcass of a stag, a deer skull ground with sandpaper and filed down so that every brittle edge was crisp and yellow. The eye-sockets were a black so deep and alive with shadow that Wendy feared looking into them for too long, although she knew she should have been able to see the man's face through them and through the gold-edged ridges of the deer's broken jaw. The antlers were tall, longer than any she had ever seen, and uneven so that all the chipped, tree-bark-grey points of one reached a little higher than the other. They sprouted from the top of the mask and splintered outward, branching into networks of spines and clawed fingers that drew shadows over his terrible non-face.

'Please,' Wendy said. 'What are you?'

'You know what I am,' said the man with the filed-bone mask. His fingers played softly on the air and he watched them with a detached kind of curiosity, like they didn't really belong to him. Particles of sand and dead skin floated around his arm as it moved. 'What are you, Wendy?'

Wendy shook her head. 'Don't do that. Answer me. Why am I walking? Where am I going?'

'I ask only a small sacrifice,' said the man in white. 'A payment of blood and time. I have asked it of others, before, and I ask it of you now. Will you pay me, Wendy?'

'Do I have a choice?'

She thought she might have sensed the man smiling, beyond his mask. 'Of course you have a choice, Wendy.' His voice was low and gruff, softer than it had been before but still undoubtedly the same. 'What kind of a god would I be if I didn't give you a choice?'

'So I can stop walking,' she said. She took a step back. 'You'll let me stop.'

Slowly, the man reached up and thin, white-laced fingers knotted around the edges of his mask. 'Of course you can stop walking,' the man said. 'And if you do, I will tear your intestines out through your anus and boil them in your own leavings at the edge of the road.'

Wendy swallowed. 'That's my choice,' she said. 'Keep walking, or die.'

'That's your choice,' the man whispered, and he removed the mask. Lowering his arms to his sides, he gripped the thing in front of his groin by the antlers, so that it looked up at her with dark, hollow eyes from between his knees.

'Oh my god...' Wendy said, raising blistered fingers to her mouth.

'Quite,' the man said. His face, his true face, revealed and brushed by the white fingers of the sun, was a horrible mess of flayed, punctured skin and tufted fur: bloody entrails drooled out of a fragmented curl of long, bear-claw teeth where his mouth should be; his eyes were a shining, translucent purple and they tumbled out of grizzled sockets in spirals and curls. A crushed, red-furred paw jutted out of his forehead like some dreadful roadkill horn and the tiny, splintered ribcage of a bird poked out of his bloody cheek. Skunk stripes peeled back from his brow and a grey-tinted tail coiled around a red, caved-in throat.

Maggots squirmed and writhed in the holes in his face and crawled between the pointed, blood-matted ears of a rotted dog. His skin – what skin there was, beyond all the sparrow bones and tangled fur – was decayed and riddled with a bruised, plague-sore coat of mortis.

Wendy closed her eyes but she could still hear him, the roadkill god with a face made of all the victims of careless tyres and hungry birds, with a voice as soft as any she had heard before: 'Walk, Wendy. Wake up and walk.'

'No,' she moaned, clapping her hands over her ears. 'No, no, no…'

'Wake up,' he repeated, and his voice had changed, no longer man or human at all but the husky growl of an animal. 'Wendy, wake *up!*'

She woke up.

For a moment Wendy laid there, on the tarmac, sobbing tearlessly. Salt-stung eyes were ringed with dehydration and her face bristled with sunburn. The electric whine hadn't stopped, wouldn't stop until she stood and kept walking. She had heard his voice now, his true voice, the voice of the roadkill god, and she knew what would happen to her if she didn't stand.

Wendy stood, legs shaking beneath her. The sky had darkened, red broken up by bands of orange and gold as the sun started to sink, dragged beneath the horizon by long, black fingers. Shadows fell over the tarmac and drifted across her feet. The raven looked up at her, a thin coil of intestine hanging off its beak.

She started to walk again, ignoring the splints of

agony in her shins. Ragged shapes lined the road ahead and the soles of her feet throbbed, wet and warm and stung.

'Come on, Freddie,' she murmured. The raven hopped alongside her as she wandered the edge of the road. The wheat-stalks drifted softly. Her throat was still dry and while the headache had faded the numbness that circled her eyes was confusing and it jarred her halfway between sleep and consciousness. Her legs moved on their own, drawing her forward awkwardly as her hips dipped lower and lower with each step. Her belly rumbled.

She walked for three hours and the hunger in her gut grew stronger, digging at her chest and the cracks of her spine. She tried to keep count of the miles she must have crossed, but the scenery hadn't changed for a day and a half; the wheat fields were relentless, crashing swathes of gold and grey that never ended, never faltered, the road never bent or curled around, never rose or dipped. Thirty miles, she thought. Forty, maybe. Christ, more. Her soles were so worn down that they slopped messily on the surface of the road – no longer was she walking on skin, or even the flesh beneath, but on bare, exposed muscles, red and raw with blood. Much further and even they would peel away and her feet would wear right down to the bones. Tarsal, metatarsal, phalanges. Or was it carpal, metacarpal, phalanges? No, that was hands, Freddie would *kill* her for making such a mockery of his career.

Freddie, she thought. She looked behind her – the raven had fallen back and he scuttled through the remains of a spiny hedgehog at the edge of the road, poking at the brown-grey stripes with his beak. They shivered about his face and he plunged his face into the poor creature's opened throat, tearing out strips of bruised, red meat.

Wendy's stomach grumbled.

'Nearly there,' she told herself, although she hadn't heard from the voice for hours. She wondered if she had ever heard it at all, or if this whole thing was just some manic construction of a mind driven insane by... by what? She was fine. Freddie always said she was a little batty but Freddie was Freddie, the golden child with the surgical degree and the master's in being-a-cocky-shithead. She would never be Freddie, even if she walked to the end of the world.

Her soles squelched on the tarmac and she squinted at a shape in the road. Not at the edge, like the others, half-buried by sand and wheat husks, but sprawled across the path with its legs splayed outward. The deer was twisted almost beyond recognition, stomach coiled around itself so that its front legs pointed away from her and its hind legs toward. It had been here for days, she realised, coming close enough to smell the reeking decay of its flesh: the fur had been scratched and scraped away and guts lay cradled in an open mess of flayed skin and broken ribs. She was a doe, and her smooth-snouted head had been crushed in so maggots crawled in deep, black cracks in her skull. Her eye was a round, shining eight-ball with a puncture right in the middle and a caved-in, amber-coloured iris.

Wendy paused. Her stomach growled again and she clutched at her belly, looking over the carcass. She looked behind her, eyes trailing into the approaching dark. The moon had risen over the crest of the end of the road and the tarmac at her back was bathed in pale silver. The deer's blood smelled like copper and raw mincemeat. She wondered if it could be all that bad. Venison, she thought. Raw venison. Roadkill venison.

Her face twisted up in disgust and she stepped past the crawling cadaver, fingers still knotted around her blouse. She couldn't believe she had even considered eating the damn thing. Oh, but she was so hungry…

Leaving the deer far behind her, Wendy carried on down the road for half an hour more before she stumbled on another body. She swayed in wild, messy zigzags across the path, leaving wet spirals of crimson behind her that glistened in the moonlight. It was a badger, belly flattened, meat pushed down into its rump and up into its neck. Without thinking she bent over the carcass and dug her hands into its middle, peeling the two bloated halves apart and scattering cracked splinters of bone over the tarmac. The badger's carcass fell apart in her hands, tender meat sliding between her fingers, slick and untouched by the sun but still warm from whatever interrupted life the animal had led. Scraps of fur plastered the muscles of the thing but she raised a handful of red to her mouth and bit down, tearing a hunk of stringy, sinuous carrion from what she could only think must be the badger's thigh.

Wet chunks slithered down her throat and she grimaced, swallowing quick enough that she might not have to consider what she was eating. She pawed at the carcass hungrily, clawing strips of flesh and bloodied organ from it and sliding them between her teeth. Slippery, bulging coils popped and sprayed the insides of her cheeks as she chewed. Her gut complained but she forced thin strings of meat into her throat until she was gagging on it and could eat no more. She stumbled to her feet and forward, never looking back at the muddied corpse, wiping blood and tufts of hair from her lips with a mucus-coated hand. Don't think about it, she told herself. Don't think about it, don't –

She doubled over, retching into the sand. Vomit crashed out of her mouth, streaked with veins of bloody red and shining, dark grey. The bile tasted of roadkill.

'You thought about it,' she moaned, wiping flecks of sick off her chin. She straightened, stepping out into the road, turned, afraid that if she stopped for too long, even to clean the chunks of meat that she'd spilled down her blouse, the roadkill god would scream in her ears and that electric whine would send her once again to sleep.

I will tear your intestines out through your anus and boil them in your own leavings at the edge of the road.

She was the badger, she thought, staggering on through the blood and the grit. Oh god, she was the badger. Behind her she heard the jackhammer pecking of Freddie's beak in the mess she'd left behind and she almost hurled again, clamping a hand over her bloody lips.

Wendy blinked.

There was somebody in the road. A little girl, blonde hair falling in beautiful curls around a round, blushing face. She couldn't have been any older than nine or ten, a small, narrow figure in the dark that seemed to glow like the moonlight had narrowed in to focus on her. Her arms hung at her sides and she wore a pretty school-dress, blue squares on white tied around her waist with a thick, pink band. An emerald-laced necklace glinted around her throat.

The little girl giggled and turned away, skipping into the wheat-field and disappearing. Wendy caught a flash of silver at the girl's toes and peered into the field, trying to follow the sound of her crackling footsteps.

'Wait!' she called, walking drunkenly forward. She scanned the field, looking for any opening the girl might have slipped through. A dozen or so feet ahead of her the wheat-stalks seemed to spread, frayed rope-ends breaking apart and scarred at their roots by dainty, silver-tipped footsteps.

Wendy looked around her and her eyes met the raven's for a fraction of a second, but she couldn't bear the look on the little beast's face and she stepped into the field.

Ground-up flakes of brittle wheat heads crumbled beneath her worn-down feet and sand and grit and dirt stung the raw mess of her soles. Every step kicked up a little dust and it filtered over her toes, drifting and singing across wafer skin and calloused, cracked nails that had been chipped and filed down by the road. She walked blind, letting the dark that slipped between the stalks slip over her; the moonlight hardly reached her, the further she ventured into the field, and she called out:

'Hello? Are you still there?'

She heard giggling up ahead, a trace echo of laughter in all the whistling of hollow reeds. She followed the sound along a ragged path in the scarred earth, hands out to the side, fingers brushing against sharp, stinging stems. Every trace of exhaustion and thirst had faded from her and the bitter, roadkill taste in her mouth seemed insignificant. I've made it, she thought.

Wendy, said the voice.

She saw the girl, again, through the stalks, skipping gleefully from one foot to the other. Golden curls flitted about her face as she turned to look back with shining, green eyes. Her skin was silvery-white and she disappeared again, fading into the shadows. Wendy walked faster, staggering almost into a run as she followed. 'Wait!' she called, but the girl would not wait.

Then the stalks peeled away and she found herself in a clearing, a sort of crop circle in all the carnage of the field. A forest glade of grey-painted sand and crushed husks. Her blood seeped into the dirt and she stood, at the edge of the circle, gentle wind whipping at the last tangles of her black-dye bun.

There, in the middle of the clearing, the girl stood beside a bent-up signpost. The grey metal was scratched at the base, long gouges torn out of it by the clawed fingers of some rabid animal, and flakes of it peeled away to reveal rough, orange patches of rust. It must have been four metres tall and Wendy found herself wondering how she hadn't seen it from the road, but then all thoughts of the road were gone, because she was staring into the face of a god.

The stag's polished skull hung at the top of the signpost, coiled antlers twisted around a rusted sign Wendy couldn't read. Moonlight glinted through three bullet holes in a smooth, white plate. The stag's eyes were hollow and she could see the stars through them; its face was a death mask of filed ivory and yellowed, narrow teeth, and its cracked jaw was bound to the post with a necklace of teeth plucked from the gums of all the creatures at the side of the road. It was crowned with a bloody ruff of fur and skin, wrapped with barbed wire so that tufts of grey and black and brown poked out and rippled in the breeze. The spines of a hedgehog splayed out behind the skull like a mess of thorns and punctured the darkness with white tips.

Bodies hung from needles jutting out of the post, rats and squirrels and flattened voles nailed there like trophies. Mangled, twisted carcasses dangled beneath the roadkill god's sleeping face and blood oozed from them as some unseen hand, the same that had pulled Wendy from her bed and along the road, squeezed their wretched guts.

The girl looked up and laid a hand on the signpost. When she spoke, she spoke with the voice of a man: the man from Wendy's dream, the faceless abomination in the white suit. 'A monument,' she said slowly. 'To me. Don't you think it's wonderful?'

Wendy nodded, eyes shifting back to the stag's head. It stared back at her, vacant and somehow hungry. Its antlers gleamed with blood.

'Come,' said the little girl, raising her hand again. Soft fingers unfurled and Wendy stepped forward. 'You have travelled far. Your pain has been recognised. Your sacrifice makes me… happy.'

'It's beautiful,' Wendy said, delirious with exhaustion. But it was, she thought, looking up at the signpost. Beady eyes glinted, crawling and writhing with maggots. Oh, Freddie, if only you could see this…

'It is, isn't it?' said the little girl. 'A truly worthy testament to my glory. You do think I'm glorious, don't

46

you, Wendy?'

Wendy turned her head, looked down on the girl. 'You were a man before. In a suit. Why do you still sound like him?'

The girl smiled. White teeth flashed in the dark. 'These roads are mine, Wendy. Everything that comes here, everything that is *killed* here…' She looked up at the creatures pinned to the signpost, eyes drooping with pity. 'They belong to me.'

The girl turned around, and Wendy saw that her back was shredded to crimson, bloody ribbons. The dress peeled away and her spine pushed up through the back of her neck, twisting at the strings of flesh that clung to it; her legs were grazed, skin worn away and muscles sheared, sprayed with grit. A long, hollow cavern of red drew chaos from her body and carved out a strip of bloody sinew from the top of her neck to the gravel-punctured mess of her legs.

When she turned again, Wendy almost forgot what she had seen. From the front, the little girl looked normal. Alive, even. Like nothing had ever happened.

'They chained her to the towbar of a Land Rover, Wendy. They looped the chains around her waist and bound her to the car while she screamed and begged them to stop. They were hardly any older; they all went to the same school.'

'Is this real?' Wendy breathed.

'They drove, and she couldn't keep up, not on her

feet. She fell, and they dragged her along the road at sixty miles an hour. They only drove for a minute, but the tarmac tore away her skin and she was dead before they hit thirty.'

'Why are you…'

'Everything,' the roadkill god said, through the mouth of the poor dead girl. 'Everything that dies on this road is mine. You do think I'm glorious, don't you, Wendy?'

Wendy nodded. She couldn't help herself.

'Then you shall be rewarded. For your sacrifice.'

Wendy took a step back. 'What do you mean?'

The little girl smiled again, reaching up to toy with the long, pink tail of a hanged rat. Blood seeped over her gentle fingers. 'Yes,' she said, 'I think you'll do.'

All at once the girl's smile fell away and her eyes darkened. Wendy staggered back but the wheat-stalks whipped at her body and something nipped at her ankle: she glanced down, saw that Freddie had followed her into the field and he was pecking at the bottom of her leg with his blood-soaked beak. Dark eyes flashed and she saw shadows writhe and twist in the dark; yellow eyes gleamed as cats and rabbits and badgers with their intestines hanging out padded softly over the sand towards her, guts dragging on the ground, blood dripping from mangled skulls and ratty, tyre-track wounds.

'Please,' Wendy whispered.

The roadkill god clicked her little-girl fingers and the *snap!* rang out in the dark.

All at once the carrion creatures closed in on her, cracked teeth clamping down on her toes and snapping at her shins. A hare with shining silver eyes and one front limb completely torn away leapt for her throat and she stumbled back, swatting away the mange-eared thing. She screamed, and her back crashed into the signpost monument as a striped cat curled its exposed spine around her shin and a flat, crisp-skinned snake hissed up at her from the sand.

She looked across at the girl and saw a chain in her hand, the same chain they had used to bind her to the back of the car that killed her.

The girl's eyes travelled from Wendy's face to the top of the signpost and she smiled, listening to the sounds of snapping teeth and tearing flesh as green-eyed death clawed at Wendy's throat. 'Oh yes, I think you'll make quite a handsome addition,' the roadkill god breathed, and she stepped up to Wendy and bound her hands above her head, pressing the chains into her flesh. The poor creatures pinned to the monument had awoken and they snapped and swung at her as the little girl looped the chains over the top of the sign and hauled her up.

'What are you...' Wendy croaked. Her shoulders sagged into the cradling antlers of the stag skull and cracked horns pierced her flesh. She could feel teeth

49

digging into her hips and her breasts and her ears, maggots crawling through her hair and into her mouth, and she gagged, drooling blood as she tried to shake herself free. 'Why are you doing this?' she screamed.

'I told you,' said the roadkill god. 'You made your sacrifice. 'This,' she whispered, stepping back to admire her handiwork, 'is your reward.'

GLIMMERMAN

1942
Cork, Ireland

A thick, glittering crust of snow crunched beneath his boots as he crossed the street. Cracked layers of ice splintered the windows of a shining, American car parked half on the kerb: a maroon red Mercury, the Marshes' proudest possession. Snow-dusted rims hung pale shadows over narrow, dark tyres. Connor Corbett had been a beat cop on these streets for six years and knew everything about everybody, and he knew that if Simon Marsh stepped outside to see his car so tainted by the late November weather before it had thawed off the paintwork, he would have a fit. Luckily, Corbett knew that Berry Marsh wouldn't let her sixty-eight year old husband out of the house in this cold, for fear his brittle bones might snap in his skin.

Corbett hopped up onto the pavement, glancing both ways down the street. He threw a jaunty wave to Mrs. Fairchild as he caught a glimpse of her trudging through the snow with her rough-coated Wolfhound pup snipping at her heels. She waved back, a smudge of blue and red in the white haze. Corbett walked quickly, gripping the black belt around his waist with one hand as he raised the other to brush half-melted flakes and ice crystals out of combed, black hair. A thin coat of stubble marred his jaw and his eyes glinted with flashes of light that bounced off the snowdust in the air. It fell all around, drifting over the shingled roofs of terraced houses and dancing between iron-bar fences.

He turned, looking up at the house. It was a narrow, semi-detached building much like many of the others along the road: the face of it was red brick and clay covered with flaking patches of plaster; the windows were dark and slips of shadow passed between dusty panes of glass. He frowned, checking the number on the gate. 64, in bold, brass letters peeling with rust. This was the place. It looked half-abandoned, thin snakes of thicket crawling up the walls and winding around the windows. The door was faded, handle brushed with snow and dark with dust. A crumpled letter poke out of a bronze slit in the wood and sagged, drooping with the weight of a thousand damp beads of dew that had half-frozen along its edges and crackled as they dripped.

'Morning, Con!' came a voice from behind him, and he turned to look over his shoulder. 'What ye doin there, kid?'

'Gas leak!' Connor called, raising his hand to the

woman across the street. She stood in the open doorway of number 61, arms folded around a grey bathrobe, curlers in her hair and faint rings of smoke drifting from an amber-lit cigarette in her mouth. Her belly hung over stubby legs and her ankles rippled out of the tops of a pair of tartan slippers. 'You know if Mrs.Dean's home? Got a call from some young lass saying she smelled gas around here, have you seen anyone?'

The woman grunted, dragging in a long sliver of tar and shaking her head. 'Nobody seen ol Mizz D for a long time, sonny. Mizral old bag musta moved away sometime before the summer, me n' my Richard think.'

'Oh, really?' Corbett said. He glanced up at the house again. Pillars of smoke rose from the crooked chimneys of the buildings up and down the street but this one was unlit. Crows pecked at the crest of the roof.

'Beats me,' the woman said. 'Never cem out all that much when she were still around. You have a good day now, kid!'

With that, she flicked the brittle embers of her cigarette into the snow and turned around, swinging the door shut behind her.

Corbett grunted, attention shifting back to number 64. He pressed on the gate and the hinges squealed as he stepped through, steel-toed boots kicking up little drifts of white as he crossed the front lawn. White clumps of powder balanced precariously on springy curls of thorn and thistle, tangled and grey as they crashed out of the grass and knotted about each other. The young man stepped up onto the doorstep and knocked, sniffing a little. Nothing, save for the cool drift of winter. He couldn't smell gas at least, not from out here.

'Mrs. Dean?' he called, knocking again. Frozen, red knuckles glanced off the wood. His tunic was damp and dusted with flakes of white that tumbled off his shoulder. He blinked snow out of his eyes and brushed himself down, slim fingers patting down dark, pleated trousers and black sleeves. Silver buttons rattled at his wrists and over a slender chest. He coughed, raising a fist to knock again. 'Hello?' he said loudly. 'Mrs. Dean, are you home? You might be in danger – if I could just come in and make sure all your gas lamps and appliances are turned off?'

He waited for half a minute before lifting his fist a fourth time.

'Try round the back!' the woman across the street yelled.

Corbett turned, saw that she had opened her door again and was standing there, one hand on the frame, gown drooping so loosely off her shoulders that he could see the sagging flesh of her chest. 'Excuse me?' he called.

'Door round the back!' the woman said. 'Ol Mizz Dean had a little cat, left the back door open sometimes so it could run in n' out. Worth a look!'

'Thank you!'

She nodded. 'Painful, watching ye stand there dripping like a wet willy,' she called.

Corbett smiled his thanks and left the doorstep, crossing the face of the house and dipping around the corner. Shadows fell over a snow-drenched path along the side of the house and he waded through tangled weeds and fallen, splintered fence-posts until he'd reached a second door near the back of the building. There was no step, just a thick white frame lined with cracks and faded paintwork that jutted out beneath the door like a slim, crumbling platform.

'Mrs. Dean?' he called again, reaching for the handle. It was stiff, but it moved with a *crack!* under his palm and the door peeled open. He paused, looking all around to make sure he wasn't being watched. He felt like an invader, stepping in without invitation. But she could be in danger. And with all these restrictions on gas (no waste, read the pastel-coloured poster in his mind, not even a glimmer) there'd be questions if he didn't get to the bottom of the leak. If there was one, he thought, stepping up onto a floor covered by sparse, thin rags of carpet. He had been called out to houses before only to discover the so-called burglary or "right weird sounds" were just kids toying with him.

The door closed and he stepped forward, drawing in a breath. No smell in this room either, except for the damp that had seeped across the walls and laid in patches over a pile of ragged clothes that had been left on a wooden worktop to dry. They had been there some time, he saw, and mould had started to spread in black spots over the cotton. The wallpaper in this dingy back room was peeling and cobwebs hung from the ceiling, thick, white tufts of webbing swaying softly from cracking plaster.

'Hello?' he said, stepping out of the room into a long, narrow hallway. He looked left (front door, shafts of light peeling through a window set into the wood; open doorway leading, presumably, to a kitchen; the foot of an ornately-carved banister, a staircase drowned in wood varnish and draped in more tattered carpeting) and right (the back of the house – nothing there save for a narrow, L-shaped lounge area bathed in shadows and a slanted cupboard beneath the stairs). 'Mrs. Dean!'

He sniffed again, and he could smell it, faint as the traces of cigarette smoke on the brittle snow outside: he fancied he could hear it hissing, a discrete, high-pitched whine right at the top of his skull. His boots squelched as he walked over the carpet and he ground them into the floor quickly, ridding them of any clinging snow before it melted into dark footprints behind him. The hallway was damp too, walls mottled with disease and corners draped in webbing. The light was dim and white where it landed on the banisters and, though his eyes had adjusted to the near-blackness of the building, Corbett struggled to see his way to the kitchen.

He had nearly reached the doorway when he heard a *thwump!* upstairs.

Corbett's head snapped around and he lurched toward the bottom of the stairs, grabbing at the banister. The sound echoed, a low hollow rattle that glanced off the walls and bounced down to the ground. 'Mrs. Dean?' he called. 'Is that you, is everything alright?'

Before he could remind himself of the gas leak in the kitchen he was halfway up, wooden slats and half-rotted boards moaning under his boots. In places the carpet was folded over and he nearly tripped, close to the top, only saving himself by clutching at the knots of the twisted pillars of the banister. He stumbled onto the landing, bare floorboards covered in dust and plagued with woodworm.

The upstairs was darker than down, slick with shadows that drizzled over the faded walls and seeped through cracks in the boards. The doorway in front of him was open and he glanced in, peering into the dark of a ruined bathroom. It smelled, musky with age and brushed with the sickly bleach smell of an open cabinet full of cleaning fluid. The mirror was cracked, splintered by the cold (god, it was *cold* up here, even colder than downstairs, and the wind seemed to whistle through the walls) so that he could only see half of a warped, broken face staring back at him. A chunk had been gnawed out of the cabinet door and rat droppings littered a stained, metal bathtub. There was a little, ragged-edged hole in the tub where it had chewed its way in and he could see it, through the hole, damp fur clinging to a rotting, shrunken carcass. The floor was smeared with urine and the piss-stench rose up in waves.

Corbett turned and crossed the landing, calling her name again. The whole house was silent, save for the shrill whistle of the weather that beat against the outer shell of the building. Maybe the woman from 61 was right, and ol Mizz D had left town. The last time Corbett had seen her she was sobbing at the train station, waving goodbye to her son. He had been there on patrol. They had barely shared glances.

He raised his hand to a cold, dust-drawn doorhandle and pushed.

Mrs. Dean's bedroom was sparse, faded light filtering in through a moth-eaten net curtain and the greasy panes of a long, narrow window. The bedframe was a gilded iron mess that dipped to one side where the feet had started to sink into the floor. The amount of decay in the building was unreal, even for a few months' worth of neglect. But Corbett's eyes daren't linger on the room for long, because he had found her.

She watched him from a faded armchair in the corner of the room, sat with her shoulders hunched forward and her grotty fingers dug into the armrests. Her eyes were coated in mucus and the whites were pallid and milky. Her teeth were gritted and her lips had been eaten away by rot so that she looked him over with a grim, shining smile. But her face was completely still, darkened by shadows and the bruises that had started to spread over her flaking skin.

Mrs. Dean had been dead for most of the summer, and the cold of the winter months had made her carcass stiff and rigid. Her clothes had pasted themselves to her chest and it sagged where the bones had started to crumble. There were no flies, not in this cold, but those that had plagued her death-chair in the hotter seasons had made easy work of her flesh, gnawing it away so that it fell off the bones of her jaw and her skull; it had turned a nasty shade of grey-green in places and in others a mangy, bloodborne red. One eye was wide and bulging and round, the other hooded with a sagging, heavy lid. Grey hair tore out of a pock-marked scalp in crackling tufts that danced in the filtered light; her fingers were no more than narrow protrusions of bone that jutted out from meat-stripped, grey hands like claws. She wore a dress that had darkened with blood and mould and beneath it, her shins had been torn up by rats so that the shadowy remnants of muscles that clung to them almost faded into the dark. She still had her black-buckled shoes on, but her ankles were so narrow, robbed of all their flesh as they were, that if her legs moved the shoes would have fallen right off her.

Corbett stepped back. She had died peacefully, he imagined, right there in the chair. Nobody had known, because nobody cared. The only ones who had known were the bloated flies that left their pulsing, white egg sacs in the hollowed-out, stringy mesh of her cheeks and the rats that had feasted on her calves. Her dress sagged over a shallow middle and he imagined that, beneath it, the skin of her belly had fallen in and pressed itself to deflated, shrivelled organs, as green and decayed as her face and throat.

Connor Corbett closed the door and stepped back onto the landing. He would have to report her dead. He wondered if her son had been killed, or if he should have someone let the poor boy know. He felt strangely detached, subdued, as though whatever damning impact the sight of the corpse had on him wouldn't set in, wouldn't really hit home, until he laid awake that night and found the image playing relentlessly before his eyes.

He remembered the gas leak halfway down the stairs, when the oily smell reached his nostrils and he realised it had grown stronger in the time he'd been upstairs. All this while gas had been spewing out into the house from the abandoned kitchen and he had been breathing the putrid stuff in, along with the meat fumes slipping off Mrs. Dean's rotting flesh. He could smell it tumbling into the hall as he reached the bottom of the stairs and he passed quickly through the doorway into the kitchen.

The room was narrow and the tiled floor was grimy, sprayed with more droppings that seemed to roll about in the shadows, tiny black pellets nibbled at by the tiny teeth of the rats that had left them. Corbett looked all around, searching for a lamp or a leaking faucet. He raised a hand to the slender, copper pipe that was pinned to the wall and stretched all around the kitchen in a dust-covered loop – stone cold. There was a gas lantern above a low, wooden cupboard but the glass casing had fallen inward and the thing looked as if it had been disconnected.

Corbett crossed the room to the stove, a dreadful thing caked in years-old rust, a squat, four-footed iron monster with a griddled face and a single black ring crowning a flat, scarred brow. The smell pushed up into his face, almost soft-fingered as it stroked his skin and pressed against the insides of his nostrils. His eyes stung with it as he leant down and reached behind the stove.

Thwump!

Corbett straightened up, spine arching in surprise. His eyes turned up to the ceiling and he waited but there was no movement, no sound at all. He had imagined it, he thought. He had spooked himself, in the empty house with the dead woman, and he was hearing noises in his damn head. Nothing up there but death, and death didn't move.

Bending down on his knees, Corbett winced as the hard floor caned his legs. He screwed up his face as he poked an arm behind the stove and fumbled for the pipes. Heat brushed his chest and cobwebs drifted in his face, sticking to the stubble around his lips. His fingers met a cool, metal valve and he started to twist –

'Up.'

Corbett froze. It was a woman's voice, not Dean but a young woman, shaking with trepidation even in the single, harsh syllable. He knew the voice: it was familiar to him, the shredded echo of a half-rid memory. Slowly, he pulled away, fingers slipping softly off the valve, and he looked up.

'You,' he breathed.

The girl pointed a shaking finger at him. 'Stand up,' she commanded, voice timid and shaking despite the attempt at authority. She was eighteen – he remembered, she had been seventeen back then and she had a winter birthday – and her dark skin was soft and smooth. She was slight, built like a fragile bird wrapped in a red knitted jumper and a scarf looped around her throat.

The smell of gas rose up all around them and he could hear it for real, now, standing so close to the leaking valve, a shrill, constant hiss quiet and subtle enough to almost go unnoticed. His heart pounded. 'What are you doing here?' he whispered.

The girl blinked.

Corbett's eyes travelled down her arm, the one hanging by her side, and he saw a book of matches knotted between her fingers. Crimson touchpaper scratched the fleshy part of her hand between thumb and forefinger and a long, pale safety match rolled between index and middle.

'You called this in,' he said quietly. 'You set the leak.'

'Surprised you didn't recognise my voice,' the girl said. Her expression never changed, eyes locked on him, mouth set in a grim scar across her face. 'Not after all that *screaming.*'

'I haven't done anything,' Corbett said. Calm, gathered, despite everything. He raised his hands and took a step away from the stove and the hissing pipe. Oil burned his nostrils. 'Roisin, please, put those down. Let's talk. Why are you doing this?'

'You *know* why,' she hissed. Tears bristled in her eyes.

He did.

'You know why I'm doing this. Why don't you say it, mister bobby-beat-cop? Why don't *you* tell me why this is happening?'

'Listen, Roisin,' he started. 'Listen, I –'

'I'm done listening,' the girl spat. She stepped closer, raising the matches. 'You remember my name, do you? Well, I remember yours, *Connor.* I've had it in my head all this time, ever since that night. Connor the policeman, the glimmerman, the filthy scoundrel *rapist* –'

'Please,' Corbett begged. Even if he shut the valve off now, it wouldn't be enough. The amount of gas in the room, in the house – god, it was almost *choking* – one glance of the match on the touchpaper would be enough to set the whole place ablaze. 'Please, Roisin, I'm sorry. I'm sorry for what I did to you, I thought you wanted it. You told me you did!'

'I told you to *stop,*' the girl said softly. 'I told you not to touch me. You just didn't *listen.*'

He remembered soft flesh in his hands. He remembered the smell of sweat and tears and the sound of sobbing as he dug his fingers into her dark, hot thighs, remembered wet teeth grazing him softly even as she cried. He remembered the gagging and the spitting, remembered smacking her square in the face when she vomited on his shoes.

'It was a mistake,' he pleaded. 'I never meant to hurt you…'

He had bent her over the railings. Shaking, dark fingers curled around iron rods and squeezed them a little harder every time he moved in her. He had never felt as strong as this, as in control. Oh, he knew everyone on these streets, but she would know him…

'My parents threw me out,' she told him. Stepping into the kitchen, plucking the match from her right hand with her left and holding it to the striking paper. Her fingers trembled in the shadows. 'I told them what had happened because I thought… I thought they might help me. I thought they might come after you. But they called me a whore and threw me out to the streets. I had to *beg* to be taken back, *bobby-beat-cop Connor.* I had to beg my own parents. Still, they wouldn't take me in. They didn't *understand,* it wasn't my fault…'

She pointed the tip of the match at his eye. Gas spread in the air all around them, thick and suffocating and draping every worktop, every surface in a shimmering haze.

'It was yours,' she hissed. 'My mother only took me back in when the police found me in an alley with a bloody metal wire in one hand and my legs open and shredded and your rotten, *stinking* foetus dead and curled up between my feet. You ruined me, Connor. You ruined my whole life, and you're going to pay for it!'

'No!' Corbett screamed, but she didn't listen to him. Quickly, she tore the head of the match along the touchpaper.

It didn't take.

'What?' she mumbled, almost dropping the thing in her haste to light it. All around them, the air hissed and glittered like oil on water. She struck the match again –

It snapped in her hand and the broken pieces tipped out of her hand and onto the tiles.

Corbett stepped forward but she raised a hand, shooting narrow eyes toward him. 'Don't you *dare,*' she hissed. Slowly, she drew another match from the book and waved it between her fingers. 'This one,' she said. 'This one seals it.'

Thwump!

Both their heads shot up as something crashed above the ceiling.

'What's that?' Roisin whispered.

'I heard it before,' Corbett said, breathless with fear. 'I thought it was you.'

She looked at him. 'It doesn't matter,' she said, after a moment. 'I came here to burn you, Connor Corbett. I came here to –'

Crreeak

Corbett swallowed. A slow, heavy footstep on rotting wood. He knew that sound, because he had heard it as his own feet hit the top step on that wretched staircase.

Crrreeeaak

'What *is* that?' Roisin said. She turned her head.

'Be quiet,' Corbett whispered. He listened over the breathing of the pipes behind him as lumbering feet moaned and wailed down the stairs. Louder every time. 'Was it just you that came? To burn me. Are you the only one that –'

The girl's head snapped round. Her eyes flashed with an anger so pure it frightened him. 'I wasn't the only one?' she said, voice crackling with fire. 'You did this to others? You weren't happy ruining one life, you had to spread your filthy seed around like… like an animal?'

Corbett swallowed. 'Did anyone else come with you, or not?'

'No,' she said flatly. 'I thought I was the only one you raped and left to rot.'

Crrreeak

Corbett reached out and grabbed the girl's arm, pulling her away from the door.

'What are you doing?' she snapped.

'Just be quiet,' Corbett whispered. He reached for his belt and gripped the handle of a slick, black truncheon. 'You didn't bring anyone else with you?'

'*No.*'

A shadow lurched across the doorway as something reached the lowest step and moved over the floorboards in the hall.

'Oh my god,' Corbett said.

The thing stepped into sight and he froze.

'It's not possible…' Roisin whispered. The matches tumbled out of her hand and clattered to the floor, spilling out of their casing in a spiral of splinters. 'How can she…'

Corbett said nothing.

Mrs. Dean stood in the doorway, one eye round and bulging, the other narrowed and pointed right at him. Her mouth had fallen open and a fat, grey tongue slipped out from between rows of exposed, tombstone teeth and the gangrenous gums they jutted out of. Even through the haze of gas that filled the room, Corbett could see clearly enough that she was far more alive than she had been five minutes ago.

'What the fuck is that?' Roisin croaked, throat clamped shut by fear.

Corbett couldn't answer. His eyes were locked on the dead thing's face, a face corroded by rot and greened by decay and yet living, breathing ragged breaths into the air before him like its dreadful owner hadn't been slumped in a chair, still, the last time he had seen her. Her feet had half-slid out of the buckled shoes and the backs were pressed down beneath bony heels wrapped in tightly-pulled flesh and drawn up to her shins with exposed tendons too chewy for the rats. She stepped into the kitchen, grinning with half her face running down her throat. Slowly, her mouth opened wide and black drool fell out of her gums.

'*Hungry*...' the dead woman whispered.

Roisin screamed.

Corbett took a staggering step back. 'It's not real,' he said, speaking more to himself than the terrified girl. 'It's a hallucination. It's the gas, it's making us see things.'

'Are you a fucking idiot?' the girl hissed, cowering behind his arm. 'We're *both* seeing it, you dumb twat! Get us out!'

'*Hungry!*'

Corbett shook his head. She smelled like the very

bowels of the house, damp and disease and mottled wallpaper all spread across her skin and smeared on the very bones that held her sagging meat together. The holes in her cheeks glistened with strings of shining, wet red that flopped about her exposed jawbone. Her bulging eye rolled madly back in her head as she took another step, letting out a long, low moan from her belly as she shuffled forward.

'Please, get us out,' Roisin begged. 'You must know how to get us out of here. You must!'

The beast swiped at his face with a bony hand and a tendon lining her forearm snapped loudly. Corbett ducked beneath the wretch's claws and winced as they grazed the top of his head. The thing's spine was showing through the damp folds of her dress and the buckshot-sprayed muscles beneath. Mould clung to her arms like moss, to the crests of her ears in ridges of furry green.

'Get us *out!*' Roisin screamed, as the rotting woman took another lunge at them and they backed into the worktop. 'Get us out, get us out, get us –'

Corbett turned and grabbed the girl by her knitted sweater, anger flashing across his face as he spat in hers. 'Shut *up!*' he yelled, and he yanked her past him into the clutches of the beast.

Mrs. Dean's gums clamped around Roisin's throat and a horrible *splotch* echoed through the kitchen as teeth untouched by decay punctured flesh and dragged a great chunk of muscle out of hr neck. Roisin screamed as blood spurted from her and dissipated in the ever-thickening haze of the air. The smell of gas was ripe and stinging but it paled in the throes of that garbage-can stink of meat and rot. Shit ran down the dead thing's legs in caked, brown streams and flaked off onto the floor and with skeletal arms she grabbed Roisin's skull and twisted it around. The girl's bloody neck tore with a *snap* and she fell to the ground, crashing to her knees on the tiles.

Corbett tumbled backward, hand over his mouth. 'I'm sorry,' he moaned, watching helplessly as the rotting woman descended on her feast of living flesh and blood, tearing at the girl's chest and digging her hands into the cavernous opening, pulling out slippery lungs and biting at the meat with a ravaging, carnivorous hunger.

Roisin was still alive, gasping for air through the shimmering, red bubbles that pooled over her lips. She blinked furiously, twitching and jerking with violent, wrenching spasms as the undead beast fed on her. Ribbons of gut were torn from her ribs and burst between the cadaver's teeth and then the beast turned her hungry eyes on Corbett and she grinned, gums red with blood.

'*Hungry…*' she moaned.

Corbett stumbled to his feet, head spinning in the thrall of the gas that seeped into his ears and nose and burrowed into his eyes. Roisin's scream rang in his head, not the scream that still echoed in the shimmering air but the *before* scream, the one that juddered and hitched every time he pulled her to him, rang in his head like the pulsing of her body and the thickening of the blood in his groin. And now he had killed her.

Now he had killed her.

Bony fingers wrapped around his ankle and yanked downward and he fell, crashing to the tiles. His head knocked a worktop as he plummeted and the cold ground smacked his belly. He swiped at the hand squeezing his calf and he dodged snapping teeth, blood and spittle spraying him as the undead beast tore at his legs. He felt warmth spread over his feet and knew that she had split the skin but his mind was so addled by fear and the pounding of his blood and the *shit-bobby-beat-rapist* stink of gas that he didn't know which leg had been torn open, only that it was one of them and it was spraying blood over her hollow, torn face. He kicked out, screeching, and his boot knocked her teeth and he backed away, hand fumbling over something long and splintered nestled in the crack between two tiles. He looked.

'Got you,' he whispered, tightening his fingers around the match as he grabbed the touchpaper with his free hand. Strong jaws clamped down on his thigh and claws dug at his groin and tore it apart through his pleated trousers, reaching in-between his legs and shredding his fleshy member, yanking the guts from him in a mess of blood and the ruptured sac of his bladder.

He didn't hear the scratch of the match-head on the touchpaper over his own screaming but heard the *whoompfh,* the awful crack of the air igniting all around him. A wave of heat rushed over his face and his skin peeled away in wet, bubbling blisters and the rotting woman, completely unfazed by the great lashing tongues of white-orange flame that tore at her bones, dipped her face into his sizzling intestines as he burned to death.

THE POSSESSION OF MATHESON KEMBLE

'Have you called him yet, Bri?' Andrew asked, sliding into a chair the other side of the kitchen table. He glanced at the newspaper spread across the wooden surface, eyes skitting over a classified ad circled in scratchy red biro.

Brian looked up from his coffee, two thick fingers curled around the handle of a mug printed with the words *Lazy Shit*. He was a broad-shouldered man, thick-set and almost seven feet tall, and the mug looked like a steaming thimble in his hand. He cocked an eyebrow, shaking his head a little as he took a sip. 'Tried,' he grunted. 'Voicemail.'

'You left a message, then?' Andrew said, reaching for the mug. Brian passed it to him and he blew on the skin of the coffee before taking a slug of his own. He clawed at the corner of a red-ringed eye, particles of sand filtering through his fingers. The coffee was sloppy and hot and Brian hadn't bothered to stir the grounds all the way in.

'Yeah, just waiting for them to get back to us now,' Brian said. 'You want breakfast?'

Andrew leaned across and kissed Brian on the cheek, brushing the taller man's skin with the ragged beginnings of a blonde, pointed beard. He smiled weakly. 'I'll eat when our lives aren't in danger,' he said. He reached up and wound skinny fingers through yellow hair, pushing it out of his eyes.

Brian frowned. His face was gruff, lined with exhaustion and set into a firm, near-emotionless square. His skin was tanned and thick, weathered from the harsh teeth of the sun and from years of working out in the forest. 'You didn't eat last night, either,' he said.

Andrew shrugged, sliding the coffee mug back across the table. Above their heads, a dusty lightbulb flickered. They paused for a second, completely frozen as if the damp buzz of the electrics had stopped time momentarily. Then the light returned to normal and Andrew said, 'Well, you haven't carved a new sculpture in three weeks. Don't start telling me to pull myself together until you head back out there and get working again.'

Brian grunted. 'Hard to find the motivation, what with all the… you know.'

Andrew glanced at the paper. 'Yeah, I know,' he said quietly. 'That's why we need this guy. If you don't hear from him by this afternoon, will you call again?'

'Of course,' Brian nodded. He stood from his chair

and the legs ground over the kitchen tiles with a loud squeal. 'Now, I'm making you breakfast and you'll damn well eat it.'

Andrew smiled, watched as his husband turned to the cupboard and began to rifle through with thick, calloused arms. He turned his attention to the newspaper, to the circled ad, and he read through it again with tired eyes as a faint drift of cold passed through the kitchen.

DO YOU WANT TO BE ON TV?

Think your best friend might be a werewolf? Worried that old coin you dug up could be haunted? Whether you're plagued by cursed objects or scared to visit your granny at the cemetery because of all the nasty zombies, Matheson Kemble has the solution to all your supernatural problems!

Matheson Kemble's Paranormal Adventures returns to television this winter, and we're looking for volunteers to appear on the show and bring all their ghosts with them! Call the number below and we'll send a team of investigators to get to the bottom of your spooky situation, and put it all on film!

'Still not sure about the guy,' Brian murmured, sliding a plate of toast – burnt at the edges, almost perfectly golden in the middle and smeared with so much butter it had started to dissolve to powder – onto the table. He laid his hands on Andrew's shoulders, rubbing them gently through the grey material of the man's shirt. Tense flesh played like knotted, damp wood beneath his fingers. 'You really think he's gonna fix this for us?'

'It's him, or the guy who wanted to charge us six grand just for a "spectral analysis".'

'And you're comfortable being on telly?'

Andrew turned, smiling up at Brian with a face paled by fear. 'Honestly, Bri,' he whispered, 'I'd be comfortable if Matheson Kemble stripped me, hung me outside the Houses of Parliament by my ankles, and made me sing *Danny Boy* on repeat if it meant I didn't have to spend another night scared for my fucking life.'

Brian leant forward and kissed him. 'I'm sorry,' he said quietly. 'Look, if this doesn't work out, we'll move. We'll find somewhere else to live.'

'With what money?' Andrew said. He blinked away a tear and shook his head, shrugging Brian's hands off his shoulders. 'And what if it follows us?'

The lights flickered again. Something crackled in the walls.

'What if it kills us before we get the chance?' Andrew moaned.

'Shh,' Brian said. 'Calm down. They'll call back. If not I'll just try again, okay? I'll keep trying. We'll figure this out, alright, and it'll all be fine. We'll be safe again.'

Brian stepped back from the table and his gaze shifted from Andrew's yellow hair to his scarred face, cheeks marred with blood, one eye a swollen, milky white where a dreadful claw had scraped the lids apart. His nose was bruised and he had tried to cover the marks on his throat with some pale kind of make-up but they showed through, slender, purple bruises that wound around his neck where the telephone cord had strangled him.

'Go on,' Andrew whispered. 'Get to work. Keep busy. I know you hate to be cooped up in here all day.'

'You could come out with me,' Brian said. 'It's not safe in here –'

'It's daytime,' Andrew said. 'It's safe. Besides, someone's gotta keep an ear on the phone.'

'You shout if anything happens.'

They kissed again, and despite the brittle scars over Andrew's lips it was warm and tender and cut off far too short by a damp, electric flutter of white and grey above their heads.

Brian left the kitchen to find his jacket, and Andrew was left alone with the fingers of the poltergeist playing on the air and a plate of untouched toast crumbling before his red-ringed eyes.

***

Brian King was shaving the pointed splinters off an owl's roughly-carved eyeballs when he heard the screaming. The light was cool and perfect, soft yellow streams crashing over the thatched roof of the cottage and spraying the yard with patches of sunshine; still, the wind was soft and cold enough that he kept the jacket on, brown leather tight and cracking over his shoulder, almost sticking to the mothball fabric of a red, checked shirt he had only bought because Andrew told him the lumberjack image would *never* be complete without it, however many pairs of chainsaw trousers and padded gloves he hung in the cupboard under the stairs.

The owl in question was a three-foot pillar of maple wood that had been stripped of its bark and worn down into harsh, angular feathers and folded wings. It was an old project that Brian had half-abandoned when the ghost first showed up; he hadn't started work on anything new in almost a month, but whittling away at the owl's curled, brown talons or the teeth of a wolf he'd left standing by the back window, he could draw out hours of the day with hardly a thought to the nightmare that lived in his house.

That first night had been one of the worst. They had a film on – a gritty, black-and-white affair from somewhere between the twenties and the sixties, a grim attempt at a horror movie where the blood was too bright, even in shades of grey, to be anything close to real, and the skin of the six-fingered monster with webbed hands and spines running down a scaly back was too rubbery to be anything but rubber. It was called *Red Weeping* or something, a classic of film which, as far as Brian could remember, was forty minutes of fake fog drenching lakeside houses on flimsy, set-piece stilts, and a further forty-five of drawn-out, laboured screams.

Then the television had switched itself off and a piercing shriek of static filled the living room. Andrew jolted out of the trance of half-sleep the dreary film had lulled into and almost leapt out of the crook of Brian's arm, looking all around the room as every single lightbulb and lampshade flickered and sizzled out and died in a blaze of orange. Brian remembered scrambling up from the sofa as the coffee table started to lift itself off the floor, top perfectly flat even though it seemed, floating twelve inches off the ground, it should at least be wobbling.

'Bri, what the fuck is that?' Andrew whispered. Then the table whipped around and everything resting on the wood crashed towards them in a blur of paper and metal. A plate shattered on the floor and a knife whistled across the crest of Brian's ear and he ducked, yanking Andrew to the floor with him. There was a *crack* as loud as thunder and he looked up, watching as a thick, black spider's web of splinters opened up in the ceiling and chunks of plaster plummeted to the floor around their heads. The sofa shot back, dragging great scars out of the floorboards and smacking the wall with a force so heavy the room seemed to shake. The television switched on again and the screen split, all at once cracking and spraying shards of glass into the room.

Then everything fell silent again and the two of them cowered, shaking, in the wreckage of the living room as the thing that had attacked them moved through to the hallway and started tossing picture frames against the walls. With every shatter of glass Andrew's whole body jolted in Brian's arms. He was sobbing.

Brian worked tirelessly, shredding peels of maple off the owl's back with a yellow-handled chisel and a hammer with a rusted head, and when the feathers had been smoothed down to the tightest strings of the twisted wood he started to slash at the corners of its eyes, rounding them into perfect spheres in the bird's heavy, wooden lids. He dug the chisel into the ring of gold around the owl's left eye and tapped lightly with the hammer, curls of pencil-shaving maple falling away and floating about his feet, and then he heard the screaming and his head whirled round.

He dropped the hammer and it crashed off his toes but the chisel stayed in his hand, locked between his fingers as they clenched into a fist. Before he could think *run* he was running, burly arms swinging at his sides as he staggered toward the house. 'Andrew!' he yelled. 'Andrew, get out of there!'

The screaming had stopped by the time he reached the front door but he could hear the crashing, tumbling carnage inside. He tried the handle but something was jamming the door from the inside, a terrible force that laid a dozen hands on the wood and pushed against it, holding it tight to the frame as Brian knocked and pounded and twisted at the handle. He yelled and took a lurching step back, raising a boot and bringing it crashing into the letterbox. The door sprung open but the force inside slammed it back and the whole frame shuddered.

'Let me in, you invisible fuck!' Brian yelled, ramming the door with his shoulder. An inch-wide gap between door and frame appeared and a sprained, red light slid out into the front yard then the ghost slammed it shut again and it crashed back into Brian's shoulder. 'Let me in!'

The third kick was enough to send the door swinging wide open and he tumbled in, wielding the yellow-handled chisel like an axe as he tore through the hallway to the kitchen. Andrew had gone – the plate of toast was still there, but the newspaper had been shredded and it lay in tattered, red-stained ribbons on the tiles.

'Andrew!' Brian yelled, glancing upstairs. He heard a crash from the bedroom and lurched up, two steps at a time, almost tripping over his feet as jagged splinters burst up out of the steps and the banisters, peeling away from the grain of the wood to jab at his ankles and eyes.

'Andrew, where are you?'

He heard a groan and stumbled into the bedroom, saw Andrew sprawled against the foot of the bed with his head lolled back, eyes half-closed as he gasped, choking on nothing as unseen fingers pulled his hair and pinned his legs, apart, to the floor. Brian caught a flash of silver in the corner of his eye and saw that a kitchen knife had lifted itself off the dressing table – Christ, the thing shouldn't even have been *upstairs* – and it hovered, trembling, in the air. Brian's eyes flitted from the knife to Andrew's exposed throat, veins bulging as he struggled for air, and he cried out as the thing flew off the desk in a streak of glinting steel.

Brian threw himself across Andrew's splayed body and the knife sheared a jagged strip out of his leather jacket. A cold spiral of air whisked at the back of his neck as it flew past and spun around, slicing again at his back as he wrapped his arms tight around Andrew and gritted his teeth. The knife slashed and spun behind him and the tip sheared a slice out of the jacket and came back to tear a frayed split in his shirt. He screamed, head bowed, as it cut his back to bloody ribbons and criss-crossed his spine. Around him mirrors and books and ceramic ornaments tumbled into the air and slammed down again in a gust of hot air and red light, crashing into pieces on the floor, and then it all stopped and the knife clattered to the floor.

Andrew's body loosened in Brian's arms and the

man breathed, shallow and rasping, in his ear, gripping the shredded remains of his jacket with shaking fingers. Brian's back was a raw mess and he hissed in agony as warmth spread over the cuts in his flesh.

'You have to call him again,' Andrew whispered.

Brian nodded and they stayed there a while, huddled in the dark beneath a blown lightbulb, and they sobbed together knowing that the poltergeist's grip on their house would return, at some point, and its rage would be relentless.

Kemble's film crew came the next day, drawing up to the cottage in a black, panelled van with a radio mast and a red-clawed werewolf painted above the wheel-arch: teeth bared, eyes yellow and ears pinned up in two jagged points, the thing screamed through a mask of cracked, peeling colours that had faded with age and dust. Next to the werewolf, printed on a backdrop of a full, pink-tinted moon, neon purple letters screamed *MATHESON KEMBLE'S PARANORMAL ADVENT*. The rest of the letters, Brian thought, standing in the doorway to watch as they began to unpack, must have worn off or been scratched off by kids young enough to appreciate the joy of committing such vandalism but mature enough to see Kemble and his show for the steaming piles of horseshit they both were.

Still, he thought, they had come – quickly, too, once he had described (in detail he hadn't been fully comfortable disclosing) Andrew's injuries. He had called them "colourful" in the hopes that a production crew might find the idea appealing. He even told the lady on the phone the spirit had plagued them for exactly twelve 'nights and that tonight was the thirteenth, in the hopes that such a ridiculous story would be what they were looking for in their next episode. They liked thirteens, Andrew had told him. He had also told him to explain that the ghost had nearly killed them both multiple times and that if Matheson Kemble didn't get his prissy shithole arse to the house then they would bring the savage poltergeist to *him* and see how he fucking liked it.

Brian had said enough to convince them, anyway.

He watched as Kemble climbed out of the passenger seat of the cab and lowered himself onto the gravel at the edge of the front yard. He was a fat little man, thinning black hair combed to one side of a shining, freckled head, with a grey goatee framing narrow, pursed lips. His eyes were hidden behind sunglasses with bright, red frames and he wore a maroon blazer brushed with deep, suede stripes. His trousers were a pus-like shade of yellow and his shirt was turquoise and frilled at the neck.

'Oh god,' Andrew said, suddenly standing behind Brian in the doorway. 'We're going to die.'

The crew followed Kemble to the front door, dragging black leather bags with them across the gravel.

There were six of them, all dressed in black polo shirts – the backs of which were embroidered, very possibly by hand, with a blazing white pentagram and the initials M.K.P.A – and black pleated trousers. A black guy with bulging muscles rippling out of his neck carried two duffel bags out of the back of the van while a scrawny, narrow-bodied man with grey skin and patchy stubble hauled a pair of tripods in his bony arms, black hair drifting in his face and a jet-black ring glinting in his right ear. A dark-skinned woman followed them with a rucksack and a bag that spilled over with lenses and sound equipment, hems of her trousers rolled up so that a pair of knitted, grey-and-pink spotted socks showed at her ankles. Between them, a red-haired man in his early twenties and a girl of roughly the same age carried an assortment of the strangest shit Brian had ever seen, all wires and monitors that looked like they'd been stripped off the boxes of ancient television sets, tumbling cascades of buttons and microphones and something he was fairly certain was a World War Two wireless with its back torn out and filled in with red cables. The sixth crewmember was a woman with blonde hair pinned back from a heavily made-up face and dark, narrowed eyes. She followed Kemble to the door, almost standing in his shadow as she held a clipboard to her chest and her heels clicked on the ground.

'Nice owl,' Kemble drawled, offering Brian a hand. It was clammy and his grip was weak enough that Brian loosened his own, fearful he might splinter the man's fingers. 'Cost you fellas much? Hell of a piece. Hell of a piece.'

Andrew smiled politely as Kemble slid his hand wetly out of Brian's and into his own. 'Oh, that's all my husband. He's an artist.'

Brian cocked an eyebrow, shooting Andrew a sidelong glance. The woman standing in Kemble's shadow sniffed.

'Forgive her,' Kemble said, rolling his eyes behind the dark lenses of his glasses. 'Pays to have a real old-testament type Christian on the team. She's a hell of an assistant – no match for Martha, the poor love, rest her soul – but she's kind of into the whole King James Bible "no gays" thing. Say husband again, she'll probably hang herself.'

Brian froze. Andrew's mouth opened, but he said nothing.

'Your faces!' Kemble screeched, and laughter slipped out of his mouth like vomit. 'Honestly, the two of you. Tell them, Karen.'

'He's joking,' Karen said flatly.

'Exactly! I'm joking,' Kemble said, 'just a joke. You mind if my boys step inside and start setting up? You two, take a walk with me. Let's go take a look at this wonderful owl of yours and talk business.'

The two of them stepped out of the door and watched as Kemble's crew dragged their shit into the front hall, followed by the stone-faced Karen and her clipboard.

'In all seriousness, though,' Kemble said quietly, 'that one really is a stone-cold bitch. She'd have the whole show shut down if I wasn't paying her double her worth.'

'Are we supposed to ask why you pay her so much?' Andrew said, following Kemble towards the owl sculpture. The red-blazered man walked with his hands slid deep into his pockets, half a head shorter than Andrew and almost completely drowned in Brian's shadow.

'Decent fuck,' Kemble said. He rapped his knuckles on the top of the maple wood owl, looking it up and down. Brian winced. 'So, boys, what can I do you for?'

Brian frowned. 'You don't know?'

Kemble grinned at him with tobacco-stained teeth. His goatee creased. 'Oh, they don't tell me anything. Karen handles the where and the when, the others follow behind and drag me along to do the talking.'

'But you can help us, right?' Andrew said.

Kemble looked him over for a moment. 'This thing's fucked you up real bad, hasn't it?' he said, tone dripping suddenly with sincerity. He looked over the deep gashes in Andrew's cheeks and shook his head. 'You were right, that is… *colourful.*'

'So how does this work?' Brian said. 'You go in, take a look around – have you got something that can stop it?'

'Tell me what we're dealing with,' Kemble said, leaning on the owl. It wobbled.

'It's a ghost,' Andrew said. 'A poltergeist, or whatever they're called. It… it's invisible. We've never seen it. But it throws things around, it…'

'It's evil,' Brian finished.

'Shit,' Kemble breathed. 'A poltergeist?'

Brian nodded. 'That's what we think. Is that –'

'A fucking *invisible ghost,*' Kemble cursed, stepping away from the owl and running a hand over his scalp. 'Do they understand television at all? Fucking imbeciles!'

'I'm sorry,' Andrew frowned, 'can you help us or not?'

Kemble turned his eyes on them and the smile returned to his face, forced this time so that his narrow lips peeled back from his yellow teeth and his eyes turned downward, just a little, dashed with anger. 'Excuse me?'

'Can you help us?'

Kemble raised an eyebrow. 'What? You two aren't serious.'

'You're *kidding* me,' Brian groaned. 'Andrew, he's a pissing fake.'

Kemble raised a hand. 'Hang on, you. Big boy. None of that. I'll have you know at least half the shit on my show is real as this beautiful sculpture here. At *least* half.'

'And the other half?'

'Well, the other half is crazy people and good acting, courtesy of myself, and I *assumed,* you know, what with the invisible ghost and all the scars on your hubbie's face – honestly, you two, those are *so* colourful they look like the best make-up job I've ever seen – I assumed the two of you had just cooked something up to get on the telly.'

'What the hell is he saying?' Andrew whispered.

'Do you know how to stop it or not?' Brian said softly.

Kemble's face hardened. 'Like I said, big boy, half the shit I've put on camera has been real. So yes, we've got the equipment to deal with this kind of thing. You think I'd spend as much money as I have developing this machinery if it was just props and toys? You think I'd hire bitch-face *Karen* if my entire life was a complete bullshit lie?'

'So help us,' Brian said.

Kemble looked at the face. Sunlight glinted off his sunglasses and drifted softly over the suede stripes on his jacket. 'Alright,' he said after a moment. 'Here's the plan. We'll get in, get the important bits out of the way – you know, the séance, the rituals, crack on all the machines and get *rid* of this thing – then I'll head home and leave the camera crew to film a couple of interviews with you fellas and get any last shots of the house. Sound good? I'll be out and done in an hour or two, the crew will be out of your hair by the end of the day.'

'And *it?*'

'The machines will sort it out,' Kemble nodded. 'If this thing is real, it's too dangerous to be left alone.'

He paused.

'I bet those scars aren't the only ones you've got, now, are they?'

Andrew glanced up at Brian.

'Show him,' Brian nodded.

Andrew lifted up his shirt, trembling fingers drawing up the material gingerly.

Four deep, crimson gashes across his belly had started to dry up and crust at the edges, yellow curls forming around long, bright stripes of raw skin where the thing had swiped at him with its invisible fingers.

Kemble swallowed. 'Okay. Well, firstly, we need to get *that* on camera. Secondly… yeah, we can sort your poltergeist problem. The machines work, trust me on that. I've only seen a couple of these fellas before, but they're real nasty shitbags. You did well to call me as soon as you did. Any longer… well,' he shrugged, 'it's a wonder the two of you have made it this long in the house with that beast.'

A silence fell over them and the air felt cooler, a draught of shadows caught on their faces and brushing their skin. The owl watched the whole exchange with blank, splintered eyes, feathered wings curled around its belly like it was sheltering itself from some dangerous thing in the air.

'Right,' Kemble grinned, clapping his hands together and marching towards the cottage. 'Let's go make some telly!'

Brian winced, gripping the edge of the bathroom sink in one hand while the other worked at the bandages plastered to his back. The old peeled off and dragged raw, wet patches of skin with them, and he tossed them in damp, red bundles into the bin beside the toilet. The new pressed tight against the rinsed gashes that crossed his spine and he grunted as the pain shot up to the top of his neck.

'How you doing there, big boy?'

Brian looked up into the mirror above the basin. Spots of red on the glass, leftovers from a smeared, ghostly handprint they had done their best to wash off, seemed to bleed out of the mess of Andrew's red-streaked face as it watched him from the doorway.

'Don't call me that,' Brian said, smiling grimly. 'In fact if you get *any* ideas from that prick downstairs –'

'Oh, don't you worry about that,' Andrew said. He stepped into the bathroom, laid a hand on the small of Brian's bare back beneath a jagged Z of peeled skin that hadn't yet been bandaged. 'You'll know he's rubbed off on me if I start wearing a striped blazer.'

It hurt to laugh, and Brian drew in air through his teeth, screwing his eyes shut momentarily. Doubled over the sink, he let Andrew finish off the bandages, tying them around his ribs and snipping off the frayed ends with a pair of rusted scissors jammed into the toothbrush mug.

'Think I might rub off on you when this whole shitstorm's finally over,' Brian grunted.

Andrew kissed the top of his head, almost standing on his tiptoes. 'Might be nice,' he whispered. 'Let's focus on today for now though, shall we?'

'Hate to interrupt a touching moment like this,' Karen said from the doorway, 'but they're ready downstairs.'

Brian turned, running a hand over his face. 'Sure,' he said, reaching for the black shirt he'd left draped over the bathtub. He shrugged it on and the two of them followed her out onto the landing in silence. Downstairs, he could hear a low, hushed chatter and the scrape of chairs dragged over kitchen tiles; a shrill hiss burst from one of the machines. The lights on the landing flickered as they walked.

'You know, I know what he's been saying about me,' Karen said as they reached the top of the stairs. She clutched the clipboard to her hip like the yellow-lined pages pinned to it contained all her darkest secrets. 'I'd ask you not to listen, but all you men –'

'Oh, we think he's a shithead,' Andrew said. 'Soon as he's fixed up our ghost problem, he's out.'

Karen smiled. The expression suited her, Brian

thought, better than the pursed, taut mask of cold non-emotion that had been plastered there since she stepped out of the van.

'You're the one who told him to come here, aren't you?' Brian said quietly.

She paused on the third step down and looked up at him. She nodded. Her eyes were ringed with pity. Her clothes were snapped tight around her angular frame but there was an air of looseness about her now that seemed to give that sharp-cornered shape a hint of warmth. 'Yes,' she said. 'Despite everything he'll tell you, I'm not heartless. We get phone calls all day, every day, from madmen and attention-seekers and potheads and sometimes, buried in all that mess, there's a case that stands out because I can hear how much it *hurts*.'

'He said something about the assistant before you – Martha?'

Karen nodded.

'What happened?' Andrew said. Below them, Kemble cursed in the kitchen as something clattered onto the table. Brian heard him snap at one of the crewmembers and a string of apologies followed.

'She told him about this case, way out towards the outskirts of London. Back when he was doing his *PSI* series.'

She looked from the blank look on Andrew's face to the cocked eyebrows on Brian's.

'*Paranormal Supernatural Investigations?* Anyway,

Martha – she was lovely, she ran the whole thing back when I was on coffee runs – found this case up in London where this woman gave birth to some kind of demon baby or something, died in childbirth, meant the dad was left alone to deal with it. Kemble thought the whole thing was horseshit, but Martha went down to see the guy on her own. Turns out the baby wasn't his, it was some kind of vampire spawn – *leeches,* Kemble calls them, I don't know if the network could ever clear copyright on "vampire" – but she got caught up in this whole mess and never came back. Just disappeared.'

'Shit,' Andrew said.

'Kemble made a two-part episode about it,' Karen said. 'Got rich enough to start a whole new series and plumb more funds into all his screwed-up ghost trapping equipment. Never spent a single penny on figuring out how to kill a leech, though.'

The two of them said nothing. Brian laid a hand on Andrew's shoulder and squeezed gently.

'Anyway,' Karen smiled. 'You two ready?'

Brian nodded.

'Good, good. And don't tell him I said any of this. He's got a very specific image of me in his head, wouldn't want to start running my mouth off all over the place.'

'"Decent fuck," I think he said.'

Karen's face flushed. 'That lying *prick.* You don't listen to a single word he says from now, okay?'

Andrew threw her a mock salute. Above his head, the lightbulb cracked and splintered. He ignored it. 'Guess we're not supposed to believe that you'd cut out our throats for being gay either, are we?'

Her face flashed still and emotionless. 'Oh no, I'll definitely cut out your throats. Even *look* like you're about to kiss in front of me and you're dead, the pair of you.'

'That was a joke?' Brian said.

'That was a joke.'

Andrew screwed up his face. 'Not a good colour on you, that one.'

'Fair enough,' Karen said. She brushed down her polo shirt and cleared her throat, arm stiffening as she brought the clipboard to her chest. 'Right, you two, let's go. Not a damn word.'

'Not a damn word,' they agreed, and they followed her down the stairs, avoiding all the cracks and splinters where the spirit had tried to drive shards of wood through Brian's flesh.

'Oh, that's not his real name, by the way,' Karen said quietly, as they reached the bottom of the stairs and she gestured them toward the kitchen.

'No shit,' Brian said. 'What is it?'

'*Keith.*'

The table was laid for a séance: Kemble's crew had draped an oily, black tablecloth over the wood and it was embroidered with blood-red symbols and signs, twisted shapes that looked like backwards-facing numbers and inverted, mix-and-match letters, all surrounding a wide, red pentagram ablaze with a selection of candles.

'You like it?' Kemble said, gesturing flamboyantly. The wireless radio had been set in the middle of it all, surrounded by flaring, waxy shafts of light, red cables trailing out of its cannibalised insides.

'What does that do?' Andrew said.

'You'll see.'

The crew stood at the edges of the room, faces drifted in the flickering shadows of bulky cameras and dangling, furry microphones. The lights had been switched off and the candlelight threw clawed shapes on the walls; on the worktop, a little television monitor had been plugged in next to the toaster, and a narrow green line thrummed erratically across the screen. Beside it, the yellow-handled chisel lay covered in toast crumbs.

'Please, gentlemen, places,' Kemble said, pulling out two chairs from the table.

'Are they filming all this?'

'Yes, yes,' Kemble said. 'And if you keep acknowledging they're there, the editing guys are going to have a really tough job on their hands, okay? Eric, grab the door, would you? There's a good lad. Alright, let's get going.'

Andrew sat, eyes darting about the blackened room. The candles smelled like sulphur and absinthe as though they'd been draped in alcohol, and thin trails of ink-black smoke wafted off their wicks, dampened by the fluttering points of white-orange light.

Brian sat beside him and squeezed Andrew's hand under the table.

'This house is plagued by a poltergeist,' Matheson Kemble drawled, plucking at his goatee with one hand as he eased himself into a chair across the table with the other. The light picked at his face; without the sunglasses, his eyes were hollow and pale grey. 'Perhaps the deadliest version of any vengeful spirit, because while they can lay a hand on our realm – flinging sharp objects about the room, smashing plates, and shredding flesh – we can never lay a hand of our own on them. They exist, as do most ghosts, in a shadowy plane between the worlds of life and death, invisible to the naked eye but not to our cameras; that's right, boys, you'll finally be able to see the face of the evil sentience that's been destroying your lives.'

He turned to the cameraman by the door, the bulky, black guy, and jerked up a thumb. The man nodded.

'Alright,' Kemble said, dropping the stage voice for a moment and leaning across the table. 'Little trade secret, we add in the ghost's face with computers. You'll never see a poltergeist on camera, boys.'

'Can we get to the bit where you get rid of him for

us?' Brian said flatly.

Kemble sat back. 'Of course, big boy,' he said. 'Good to go, Eric?'

Eric – the scrawny kid with the tripod – nodded.

'Alright, let's join hands,' Kemble told them, laying his arms flat on the table so that his palms faced upward and his fingers curled in a little. Andrew took his right, and Brian his left, and they raised their interlocked hands so that they rested on the oily cloth. Between them, the wireless radio and the candles were drenched in shadow.

'What now?' Andrew said.

'Now, we call him to us,' Kemble said. And then, louder, turning his bearded chin upward and squeezing their hands, 'O, wandering spirit! We beg a visitation upon your lost soul, will you grant this to us? Spirit, show us your face! Speak to us, of your unfinished business and the tether joining your plane of death to our own! Speak to us, poltergeist!'

The wireless crackled.

'What the…'

'Speak to us!' Kemble said, yelling suddenly, crying into the candlesmoke. 'Spirit, bless us with your presence! You are here in this house, you have made residence here, so come to us, we beg, and share your unearthly face with us! *Venit, exspiravit!* Come, ghost! *Venit sedens super faciem meam!* Come, show your face to mine!'

Sparks shot off the red wires jammed into the back of the mahogany-framed radio and Brian jolted backward, letting go of Kemble's hand. He grabbed at it again and watched as static started to hiss from the thing's speaker and a voice played through it, filtered through the haze of the candlelight:

Matheson Kemble, it said. *You again.*

'Again?' Kemble said dramatically. 'Spirit, have we met?'

You think you can banish me to Hell and not expect repercussions, mortal? You think you can violate *me and go unpunished?*

The voice was cold and harsh and it dragged through the speakers like silt, crashing into the room with an echo.

'But why these men, spirit? Why harm them?'

No more questions, mortal! the voice cried, and all at once the candles were blown out by some unseen force and the room was pitched into shadow; red lights crashed up from beneath the table and Kemble's head shot back, neck exposed. His eyes rolled up into his head and the hands gripping Brian's and Andrew's tightened into claws. The man screamed as his knees flew up to crash against the underside of the table and his chair tumbled back – he let go of their hands and fell, smacking the back of his skull on the wall. Brian stumbled out of his chair and crossed the table, calling out the man's name as a seizure gripped his body.

Kemble's arms and legs twitched and jerked with violent, rocking spasms and he gurgled in his throat, clutching at his chest with knotted fingers. 'I... remember... you...' he spat. Brian staggered back as Kemble shrieked, rocking and swaying on the floor.

'You're fucking kidding me,' Andrew said behind him.

Brian turned, frowning.

Andrew had stood up and he held something in his hand, a red lightbulb set into a little black disc. Slowly, he flicked a switch on the side of the thing and the light blinked off, on, off.

'What the fuck is that?' Brian yelled over the hissing from the wireless. Below him, Kemble had stopped convulsing.

'Cut!' Kemble yelled, waving his arm. 'Cut, cut,' then, turning his face to Brian, 'what the fuck do you think you're doing?'

He stood, suddenly, brushing himself off, and leaned across the table to snatch the bulb from Andrew's hand.

'They're taped all along the bottom of the table,' Andrew said bluntly. 'Brian, he's playing us. This whole thing, it's a joke.'

Brian looked from Kemble to the mess of blown-out candles and red cables on the cloth-covered table. 'Turn the lights on,' he said quietly.

'Listen,' Kemble said, 'I don't think –'

'Turn the lights on!' Brian yelled, shooting a look

towards the scrawny guy with the boom microphone. Eric scrambled backward and flicked on the lights. The kitchen was bathed in yellow and Brian knelt down, peeling back the cloth beneath. A circle of red bulbs had been gummed to the wood.

'He's a fraud,' Andrew said quietly. 'He can't help us at all.'

Brian reached across to the wireless and spun it around, digging through the red cables with his fingers. He found a button and jabbed it.

'You think you can banish me to Hell and not expect repercussions, mortal?' said a pre-recorded voice from deep in the belly of the wireless. 'You think you can violate me and go unpunished?'

Brian turned on Kemble and his eyes were dark with anger.

'Everybody out,' Kemble said quietly. 'Leave me with the boys for a second, would you?'

The door opened and the crew tumbled out, taking their cameras with them. The boom mike hit the doorframe on their way out and it closed behind them.

'Listen,' Kemble said, taking a step back. He scratched at the top of his head. 'The machines work. That one, over there,' he insisted, jabbing a finger toward the little monitor on the worktop, 'that's clearing the air of spiritual energy right now. We've set up a whole mess of electronics in your living room that will, quite literally, *suck the ghost out of your house.*

Honest to god, all that part of it works. But that doesn't make good telly, see?'

'So while your machines – maybe – do the hard work for you,' Brian growled, 'you keep us in here and put on a show?'

'Exactly,' Kemble nodded. 'Exactly. We're not tricking you, see, we really are working on getting rid of this spirit –'

'But you wanted to make us look like idiots in the meantime, *Keith?*' Andrew spat.

'No! No, we just have to make it look good!' Kemble said. He backed towards the door as Brian stepped towards him. 'Honest, how many viewers do you think we'd get if the whole show was just blinking lights and computer screens and a little fancy keyboard work? Karen's in that room right now fixing your ghost problem right up, I promise! Look, if you gents would just take a moment and think about this – why don't we go make sure the ghost is gone, yeah? We can go check up on her, see how she's doing, and then we can come back to this and just shoot a few scenes of quality television. How about that, huh?'

Kemble turned and pulled at the doorhandle. It didn't open.

'Guys?' he called. 'Have you locked us in here?'

'There isn't a lock,' Andrew said quietly.

Brian swallowed. 'It's here,' he whispered.

'What?' Kemble yelled, yanking and twisting at the

handle. 'Guys? Get us out of here!'

Brian gripped Andrew's hand. Behind them, the wireless spat static. 'No more questions, mortal,' it said. Caught on repeat, the voice grew higher in pitch with every burst of noise: 'No more questions, mortal. No more *questions, mortal. No more QUESTIONS, MORTAL.*'

'Turn that fucking thing off!' Kemble yelled. He kicked at the door but it didn't budge an inch and he stumbled back. 'What the fuck is happening? Karen, tell me those machines are doing their *fucking* job!'

Brian heard a muffled yell from the other room but he couldn't make out the words. Behind him, all the dials on the oven spun to full with a *clack-clack-clack* and a burst of heat crashed out of the door as it swung open. The toaster handle slid up and down so forcefully the thing tipped up on its plastic feet and its metal-grille insides spilled out and clattered over the worktop.

'What the *fuck* is happening?' Kemble yelled. His eyes turned to something on the counter and widened.

Brian followed the direction of the little man's gaze and swore.

The yellow-handled chisel had stood up on its shaft so that the blade, a long, filed rectangle with a sharpened edge and a dreadful silver glint to it, pointed straight up. The chisel twirled slowly on its end, shining in the light as it performed a cruel, twisted dance on the marble.

Kemble looked from the chisel to the terrified couple and shook his head. 'This is all it does?' he said. 'It takes... things, and makes them *spin?*'

He laughed.

Brian's eyes were fixed on the spinning chisel so he didn't know anything had happened until Andrew screamed beside him. Then his head snapped round and he looked in Kemble's direction, watched with horror as invisible fingers grabbed the lapels of his jacket and yanked him to the counter, dragging him six inches into the air and smacking his gut into the edge of the marble surface. Kemble cried out and doubled over, hands gripping the counter, wide eyes on the chisel barely a foot from his face.

'No,' he moaned, then the spirit grabbed his hair and pulled it upward with such brutal force Brian heard his scalp tearing. The chisel stopped spinning, a flat blade pointed at the ceiling and absolutely still, and Kemble tore at the hands holding him in place but his curled fingers grabbed at the air and found nothing. 'Help me!' he yelled. 'Don't just stand there, fucking help me!'

The ghost thrust Kemble's head downward and the chisel ploughed through his eyeball in a spray of crimson and white, plunging deep into his skull. Kemble stumbled back and the chisel came back with him, bright yellow handle poking out of his face.

'I'm sorry!' Kemble screamed, but the poltergeist wasn't finished with him. Brian raised a hand to his mouth as bile tore up his throat, unable to take his eyes off the man even as the spirit lifted him into the air and dragged the chisel out of his skull with a long, slow *shiiick.*

'Put him down!' Andrew yelled. 'Please!'

Brian heard more yelling from the hallway but he could say nothing, do nothing, just watched as ghostly fingers twirled the chisel in front of Kemble's face.

Then a voice from the wireless, not the pre-recorded voice of the fraudster but a new one, shrill and wicked and gleeful. It said, *Blinding show, Keith!* and giggled like a giddy child as it thrust the chisel forward and screwed it into his good eyeball. Gelatinous, white mess drizzled down his face and he screamed again.

Suddenly Kemble crashed to the floor and his arms were wrenched upward – the sleeves of his ridiculous jacket tore first, separating from the blazer with a hiss of pulled stitches, and then his limbs were pulled clean off his shoulders in a bloody *splotch* of shredded muscle and popped bones. Kemble had passed out but it didn't stop his mouth opening, jaw yanked so far down from his skull that it snapped off and dangled, bloody, as red gushed out of his mouth and spilled onto the tiles. His broken jawbone jerked up and down like the wooden chin of a ventriloquist's dummy in time with the laughter crackling from the wireless and then his chest burst open beneath his frilly shirt and the blue turned red with blood.

His body smacked the floor and long, invisible fingers yanked down his soiled trousers and plunged sick claws into the flesh of his back, digging out flesh and tossing it across the tiles and pulling out great coils of shining entrail from beneath a spine that it twisted carelessly and wrenched out of his carcass altogether.

Andrew sobbed, and the voice from the wireless laughed with some sadistic, child-like joy. *You next!* it screeched, and the red bulbs beneath the table shattered, one by one, spraying shards of tinted glass on the floor. The whole kitchen turned itself upside down and the candles lit in a screaming mess of sulphur and streaming, white flame, and Andrew held Brian's hand tight as the spirit threw them across the room and started work flaying their skin.

Outside, the carved maple owl watched the house with scratched-out eyes. Somewhere in the back of the black van on the drive, a machine that Eric had forgotten to bring into the house blinked, and an error message flashed up on a tiny, black screen.

The message said:

nice.try.keith. :)

The screen flickered, died, and splintered with a *crack*. The van fell silent.

Inside the cottage, somebody screamed.

SKIN

The tent casts a shadow over clipped blades of grass and cracked earth. It lays six miles from the nearest town, a small settlement called Clay Hill erected in the late eighteenth century on the site of the infamous Tracey Twins Murder and populated by a little over sixteen-hundred men, women and children. Legend says the ground at Clay Hill has been soiled over the last quarter-century by the hastily-buried corpses of the twins, who haunt the town and the surrounding hamlets with restless, relentless abandon. Legend also says that their killer, the inherently-villainous cannibal Douglas Child, who hanged himself shortly after butchering the children and feasting on their kidneys and livers, wanders the streets as a wraith with a broken neck and piercing blue eyes.

Only half of all legends, as Thomas Randall knows, are right.

He watches from the other side of a wide, winding footpath as people flock to the tent, walking excitedly from the town and passing through a great red flap of an entrance strung with fluttering bunting flags and fairy lights that crackle blue, green and gold. Sheltered in the shade of his four-by-four, he stands with his hands in the pockets of a long, black coat buttoned around his belly and a flatcap tipped so far forward that it covers his eyes in shadow. White teeth flash between narrowed lips as he grimaces. The air smells like smoke and popcorn.

Around the back of the tent, a fat woman in a high-viz jacket directs trailers and campervans to an overflow parking lawn fenced off with rows of young, scrawny apple trees. She smiles all the while, round cheeks red with the lashing of a cautious wind, eyes hidden by round glasses. She is the whore's mother.

A family of six enter the tent, greeted by an equally-fat man in a suit and tie with a black moustache that curls up in greasy spirals from beneath a chunky, crooked nose. He hands a pamphlet to everyone who passes beneath the fairy lights, grinning with a sickly-friendly face as they hand him coins, notes, whatever they have in their pockets. Some give nothing, because they can afford nothing. He lets them in nonetheless. Others have fifty-pound notes in their coats and they hand them over without complaint because they're certain it'll put them on some kind of internal shortlist. Like the fat man in the suit will be able to remember every face and tell his daughter who to call up to her little wooden stage. *Pick that one,* he says, *he slipped me a crisp hundred.*

But what about the poor, frail old man in the wheelchair, daddy?

He gave me shit all, he can fuck himself.

Thomas Randall peels open a tab of caffeine pills from inside his coat and pops three in his mouth, blinking away a crust of salt from tired eyes. The tent is erected every sixteen days, always in the same spot and always for exactly twenty-four hours. Then the whole thing – a glorious, black-and-white striped affair the size of a small house – is taken down again, a marquee framework of scaffolding stripped away and the entire tent folded into bags and driven back home.

The fat man, of course, is the whore's father.

Randall hasn't slept in twenty-eight hours. He has eaten well, out of excitement, but his nights have been spent preparing. This cannot go wrong.

It won't, he thinks to himself. The cannibal Douglas Child was a coward, and his victims were children. Weak, timid children who had done nothing to him save to be in the wrong place at the wrong time. Thomas Randall is no coward. He is strong, strong with all the force of the Babylon Flower and willing, willing in absolution to do anything in his power to stop her.

The whore's father smiles at a young man in a brown coat, clapping him on the arm with one sausage-fingered hand as he accepts a handful of copper change with the other. The young man steps into the tent and disappears. The whore's father straightens his tie.

Above the tent, the sky darkens a little; a storm lingers on the horizon, brushing a sun-stroked treeline with arcs of intermittent lightning and a haze of rain.

Thomas Randall counts to ten before crossing the footpath and joining the back of the queue, reaching into his pinned-up jacket for a crumpled twenty.

Dolly sits behind a bright, red curtain hung over the stage and listens as they trawl into the tent. Her head throbs with the first push of a headache she knows will last, now, for somewhere between four and six hours, no matter how much water she drinks or painkillers she chucks down. She looks into a mirror in her lap, an old-timey kind of thing with a pearl handle and rhinestones glittering about a pale green frame. Her face is made-up as subtly as her mother would allow; she likes it more colourful, says all the men'll stop coming if she doesn't pretty herself up for them. Dolly reminds her, almost daily, that she's eighteen and half the men that come to the tent are either almost too old to be living or too fragile to walk her home. Plus, she says, you know how it never ends well with me and boys. Her mother looks at her sometimes and frowns, just a little, just for a moment, like she isn't sure what she's looking at.

The girl is beautiful, undeniably, brown hair almost shining around a slim, delicate face. She's dressed in a plain blue t-shirt and dungarees pinned to her shoulders and rolled up at the heels; the necklace her gran left behind tapers around a slender throat and a single, silver ring decorates her left index finger. She smiles into the mirror and slides it away from her on a makeshift dressing table. She sighs, glancing up at a little clock her father has hung from the scaffolding at the back of the tent.

Nearly time.

Dolly stands, brushing her hair out of glancing, green eyes and turning to face the curtain. When it lifts, she'll smile, gleaming into the expectant faces of two-hundred visitors. Some she'll recognise, because they come every time, waiting for the day when it's their turn to come up onto the stage with her. Some are new. They smile up at her with eyes so wide they look like little puppies, and she hates it. She hates the fact her dad named her after a singer, hates the fact the air in the tent gets so damn hot so quickly, that it always smells like popcorn (Sheryl and Donald Stett bought it back in 2006 after the Clay Hill Circus Spectacular shut down, and the stink lingers on the canvas like a bunch of clowns clambered up to the very pointed tip of the thing and rubbed butter and salt all over it) and that every sixteen days they make her stand up there and disappoint a hundred and ninety-nine people just to fix one broken arm.

Still, she blinks herself into a false smile and stands,

hands by her sides, counting down the last seconds until the chatter starts to die down and her father's footsteps ring out on the stage the other side of the curtain, unseen but felt in tremors in the wooden boards, and shouts:

'Welcome, one and all! Thank you, thank you for coming, now who's ready to be *saved?*'

Dolly's smile almost becomes real for a second. Her father practices, sometimes, in the bathroom, and she and her mother listen from the living room as he calls out to the glass mirror and waves his arms like a madman.

There's a cheer from the crowd, a low moaning celebration of the now-familiar opening line, but it isn't enough. It's never enough.

'I can't hear you!' Donald Stett calls. 'I said, *who's ready to be saved?*'

The cheer is louder the second time and the curtains are drawn up into the roof of the old circus tent. Her eyes turn up as she steps forward and they drift over a spiralling funnel of canvas dotted with sunlight filtering through from above. Her father shoots her a smile, the proudest, most loving smile she's ever seen, and she smiles back before turning her attention to the crowd. They fall silent as she steps right into the middle of the stage, clipped heels *click*ing with every slight step.

She looks around, across withered faces and bright, young eyes, walking canes and bandages and skin crashing with scars or spots of cancer or the wrinkles of age. From the back of the tent a deep, wet cough breaks the silence. Beside her, her father steps back into the shadows and her mother, high-viz jacket wrapped around her waist, squeezes his hand.

'Hi, everyone,' Dolly says, raising a hand.

This time the cheering is real, not some laboured response to a showman's patter but a real, cascading round of love and joy and appreciation. There is applause, soft at first but spreading with a ripple through the heart of the crowd, tumbling over plastic chairs and brittle, sun-deprived grass; there are catcalls and whistles and professions of want and need and lust. The celebration isn't for her, she knows that, but for the gift. The want, the need... they are for the power, not the wielder of it. The lust is a lust to be healed.

The crowd is divided in two, rows of chairs split right down the middle by an aisle wide enough for two people to pass. There used to be cushions, set at the front, for kids to sit closer to the stage, but she couldn't bear to look them in the eyes and not touch every single one of them with her gift, so the cushions went away.

She looks all the crowd over, raising a hand again for quiet. 'It is so good to see you,' she says. She speak quietly, but the silence in the tent is so thick she knows even those sat right at the back can hear her clear as day. Still, the words feel unnatural, rehearsed and fraudulent. Not her own. 'Welcome, all of you. I have to say... the same as I say every time, the same as I wish I could say every day... I have to say I'm sorry that I cannot do more. I wish I could fix every broken body, mend every shattered soul... I am only sorry that, today, as always, there will be only one.'

The silence is deafening now. It is a silence of waiting, of anxiety and anticipation. The air is dense with popcorn-smell and sweat. Her eyes pass over pleading expressions and she swallows her guilt. For a moment her gaze halts on a man in the front row, seated at the end of the line so that his foot dangles in the aisle. His leg quivers up and down nervously, dressed in slim, black jeans faded at the knees. He is wearing a brown coat and he looks her age, or thereabouts – he can't be any older than twenty, she thinks. And he's attractive, a crisp jawline clean-shaven and tanned beneath thick, curly hair that falls in his eyes. And he looks at her, and she looks at him, and for the slimmest fraction of a second there's something there between them that Dolly has never felt before.

Her eyes shift to a woman in the third row back from the front and she points. 'You,' she says quietly. Her heart sinks a little. She can't look at him again. All she can do is applaud with the others as the woman in the third row stands on her feet and walks, starstruck, down the aisle.

She is middle-aged, probably forty or forty-five, and her brown hair drifts in luxurious curls over a forehead plastered with little beads of sweat. A summer dress clings to a perfectly-curved body and she walks with purpose, some gleeful determination that Dolly only wishes she could feel for herself. She beckons the woman to a little set of crooked stairs at the edge of the stage and helps her up.

'What's your name?' Dolly says, gripping the woman's hand.

'Mavis,' the woman says, looking out over the crowd. Her eyes are grey and brimming with tears. 'Mavis Johnson. I'm so… I'm so grateful to be here. Thank you, Ms. Stett. You won't regret picking me, I promise you that. Oh, thank you, Dolly. Thank you.'

Dolly glances back at the crowd. A sea of silent faces watches the stage. Some shake their heads, bitter with disappointment. Others lean forward, still anxious to see the gift at work. Some, indifferent now that they know today is not their day, simply watch with dull eyes.

The young man in the brown coat watches eagerly, with a joy at the good fortune of Mavis Johnson so pure and honest that Dolly's heart breaks for him.

Dolly turns back to Mavis and smiles. 'Mavis Johnson,' she says, loud enough that everybody can hear. She grasps both the woman's hands and squeezes them. From the side of the stage, her parents watch and hardly dare to breathe between them. 'What can I do for you?'

Mavis swallows, glancing from Dolly to the crowd

and back again. Slowly, she peels her hands away and lifts them to her head. With trembling fingers the woman tugs her curled hair upwards and pulls it off.

She lowers the wig to her belly and holds it there, head bowed a little so that everybody can see the bald scalp beneath. Someone in the audience gasps.

'It happened in a motorcycle accident,' Mavis says. 'I was knocked right off the back of my husband's bike by a car, going double the limit. I… fell, broke it open on the tarmac. The doctors, they did the best they could, but my husband… he won't look at me anymore. The wig helps, but I have to take it off at night and he turns away, doesn't touch me. He doesn't love me, not like he did before.'

'It's okay,' Dolly says. She stares at the top of the woman's head, quite unable, despite herself, to take her eyes off it. 'It's okay.'

The woman's crown is a mess of patched-up skin, sewn together in quilted squares of tainted red and pallid grey. Beneath the stitches blood bubbles through in tiny beads, glittering in the lights of a thousand fairy bulbs strewn around the ring of the tent: each bead of blood glistens with a perfect, yellow-pus shell. The edges at the top of Mavis' brow and above her ears are red and raw. The colouration of the individual skin grafts is mismatched and uneven and some of the patches shine with sweat while others look thin and half-dead. One square of skin almost the same colour as the woman's real face is so blotchy and puffy with bubbles of trapped air that it looks set to burst with the slightest prick of a needle and spill out all the blood beneath. Her skull is caved in at the back so, without the wig, her head looks entirely the wrong shape, too squat and almost fluid to be real.

'Come,' Dolly says, extending her hands. She closes her eyes, but she can't blot out the image of all that fused, discoloured skin and the deformed shape of the woman's skull. 'Come, take my hands, and be healed.'

Mavis drops the wig and Dolly feels clammy fingers in her own, starts to squeeze them. She focuses, all her concentration on the single word *fix* repeated again and again in her mind and she feels it, flowing through the veins in her arms to burn at the very tips of her fingers, a gift so true and so powerful that she feels blessed despite the pain she feels, suddenly, at the back of her head, as if someone has taken a hammer and smashed in her skull –

'Whore!' yells a voice in the crowd.

Dolly's eyes snap open and she looks around. Mavis, half-healed, lets go of her hands and gasps. It all happens in a few seconds and Dolly can hardly react but in that moment, before the nightmare begins, as her head turns toward the audience, she catches a glimpse of Mavis' half-healed head, a curved crown of bone poking up through her skin and softened, squishy, a mesh of white and grey slick with blood.

The man rears up from the back row and staggers into the aisle, pulling open a long, black coat to reveal his chest. He is slender and his ribs poke up through his skin; there is no shirt, and all his chest hair has been shaved away to reveal a bloody symbol carved into the flesh between his nipples. The symbol looks like a rose, petals all splayed with crusted red skin, and the blood has dried to almost-black so that the rose sprouts out of a thorny branch curled into a spiral that loops between the petals and knots back on itself. He screams, an animal roar so dreadful and tight with rage that Dolly staggers back on the stage.

He pulls a gun.

'Whore!' he yells again. 'Filthy fucking whore of revelation, with all the strength of the Babylon Flower I have been sent here to kill you before you bring the end of our world, and so help my soul I will *do as the Flower commands!*'

Time seems to slow down as he points the gun up at her face and squeezes the trigger with a shaking, bony finger. Dolly cries out as a blur of brown and black flies into the aisle and stumbles back – the *crack!* comes almost a second after the gunshot but the bullet passes through blood and bone and the folds of a brown coat before Dolly can blink and she screams – and the young man in the front row falls, the hole in his chest spewing thick, red blood onto his shirt and the bigger, more savage hole in his back leaks onto the grass as he lies

118

on his spine and gurgles.

Dolly stumbles to the stairs, head thumping, blood thick in her ears, lurches down them with a sickness brewing in her throat. She hears screams, all through the tent, vaguely recognises that two burly men have grabbed the figure with the black coat and the flower carved into his chest and they're dragging him out of the tent, but all she sees is the dead man in the grass through a haze of her own tears.

'No!' she sobs, kneeling over him. It replays in her mind, the image of her saviour leaping out of his chair and into the aisle to catch the bullet with his ribs, like she missed something on the first watch and can't help but jam her finger on the remote again and again and again. 'No!'

Behind her, Donald Stett beckons everyone out of their seats and towards the exit, scrambling madly as her mother bounds up to her side and clutches at her hands.

'Baby,' Sheryl moans, 'baby, baby, come away, please…'

Dolly lays a hand on the young man's chest and blood pools over her fingers. It's warm, still throbbing. He looks almost peaceful, one arm resting softly on his gut, eyes closed and hair drifting over them, glinted with gold from the peeling sunlight and the shadow-speckled canvas walls.

'I can help him,' Dolly breathes. Around her the

carnage spreads in a chaotic mess of screaming and pounding footfalls, but all she can see is his peaceful face and the blood between her fingers. She can see his heart, through the hole in his sternum between her index and middle finger, and she balks. It pulses, twitches once more, and stops altogether. A still, wet sac of purple in a mutilated ribcage stuck through with shivers of splintered bone.

'Baby, you've never... he's dead,' her mother insists. 'You've never brought anyone back from... that, before.'

Outside, the black-coated man is pressed against the side of a van and his gun is tossed to the floor. Somebody runs. The screaming turns to sobbing and the man shrieks about a Babylon flower and a prophesy to stop the end of the world. Someone punches him in the face.

'I can do it,' Dolly says. 'I know I can. I just have to have faith.'

She closes her eyes, lays both hands on his chest. She *feels*.

'Baby, please,' Sheryl says. Dolly shrugs off her hand and shakes her head. 'Baby, it could *kill* you...'

Dolly concentrates. She feels the dry grass poke at her knees through the denim that covers them, feels the cold rings of the buttons pressing against her chest. She feels warm blood on her palms and digs her fingers into his shirt. She doesn't even know his name, but he saved her life. Popcorn and smoke. Whore! Perfect eyes, closed in death, but the way he had looked at her…

There's a *pop!* and the flesh starts to knit together beneath her fingers. She hisses, gritting her teeth as pangs of agony slice at her heart. They cut deeper and twist inside her chest as the mess of his swells up and heals itself. It feels incredible, like sex and relief and *power,* the gift courses through her and leaves her fingertips in a beautiful surge of ecstasy and the pain spreads across her back as an invisible bullet smacks her breast and passes through, knocking all the air out of her —

He gasps.

Dolly opens her eyes, clutching at her heart with a bloody hand. She looks down at him. He blinks madly, scrambling to his knees. Sheryl holds his arm steady.

'It worked,' Dolly breathes, and then she leans forward and wraps her arms around him in a tight embrace. He hesitates before laying his hands on her back and pulling her tight.

There's blood everywhere.

After a moment she pulls away, smiling from ear to ear. The young man smiles back, looks from her to her mother and down at his chest.

'Baby, you did it,' Sheryl says, kissing her daughter on the forehead and standing. 'I need to find your father. You two, stay right here.;

They look at each other for a moment. He opens his

mouth to speak, and then shuts it again.

'How do you feel?' Dolly says.

He smiles. He reaches for her hand, slick with blood, and squeezes it in thanks. Then he says, 'Hey, whatever the fuck just happened… do you want to grab a drink with me tonight?'

He presses her to the bedroom wall and they kiss in a ravenous, glorious mess of hot breath and skin. His hands are everywhere and hers curl into the small of his back, digging her nails into his skin as she pulls him close.

'You're incredible,' he breathes, right in her ear, voice so soft it makes her tremble. Eyes closed, she raises her arms and he lays his lips on her neck, only breaking away when his fumbling hands draw her t-shirt up over her head and his hands return to her hips.

'The bed,' Dolly moans. 'Please.'

He – Frank, his name is Frank – pulls Dolly on top of him and she looks down, hair falling in her eyes as she smiles. Her hands explore his chest and she tugs at his shirt. He glances down at it, drawing her hand to his mouth and kissing the tip of his finger.

'Off,' she says.

Frank nods, frantically pulling it over his tousled hair and tossing it to the end of the bed. Her sheets are fluffy and covered with roses. She clambers awkwardly off him and the dungarees fall to her ankles. She steps out of them and grins as she catches him tracing lines over her bare, narrow legs, and then she climbs back on and straddles his waist and plunges down to kiss him again.

'Why did you come?' she whispers into soft, strong lips.

He frowns into the kiss, hands roaming her thighs. 'Excuse me?'

'To the tent,' she whispers. 'Why did you come to the tent?'

He hesitates.

Dolly sits up, slapping away the fingers that have curled around the hem of her knickers and folding her arms over her chest. 'Hey,' she says, pouting a little. 'You have to tell me.'

'Cancer,' Frank says quietly. His expression sags. 'I have cancer.'

'Not anymore, you don't,' Dolly says, and she leans down to kiss him again.

When he's inside her she feels everything; she doesn't mean to, not this time, but she revels in it anyway. The gift courses through her blood like a drug, like the twisted roots of some deep-seeded plant curling and writhing around her veins and digging perfect, shining thorns into her flesh. She feels his heartbeat, refreshed and perfect, feels the tumours clinging to his lungs and feels them start to shrivel and fade away, feels his grief and his guilt and sees, through his eyes, blinking hospital lights. He groans beneath her and they connect, through flesh and passion and through the power drifting from her fingertips to his tangled hair and his throat, and as they finish together she feels it twice over.

Frank lets out a strangled gasp and spasms beneath her, suddenly clutching her hips with tight, frantic hands. Dolly cries out in pain as his nails dig into her skin and she opens her eyes to look at him, heart pounding with fear.

'What's happening to me?' he screams, but it's too late, she can't stop it. The gift floods through her fingertips in an uncontrollable, crashing wave and his skin bristles, hairs standing on end all over his body. She tries to pull away but she's trapped, frozen, helpless but to watch.

It starts with his arms and legs, spasming and wrenching violently as the skin begins to peel away and flake off in great strips and thick, fleshy sheets, curling and tumbling into the bed. Blood streams through rivulets in his exposed muscles and his nails tumble out of his fingers and he howls, chest jerking wildly. He clutches at her but she swipes him away, terrified and wide-eyed, covered in blood and mucus, stumbling off him and off the bed. 'Mummy!' she screams. 'Mum, dad! Please!'

Frank sits up, arms red and lined with creases, bones showing in flashes of white through gaps in the muscles and tendons that cling to his skeleton. Skin falls from his legs to the floor and his bony knees point upward, bloody but pale as the walls. It reaches his groin and his chest and the screaming stops as his flesh tears itself away from his gut with a sound like ripping paper, and then the red death reaches his throat and he tilts his head back as his face is wrenched off his skull. Muscles pulse at the corners of his mouth and he gasps, gargles, then round, bulging eyeballs pop in their sockets and he falls back, hitting the sheets with a dreadful, wet *splat*.

Skinned, Frank lies still on the bed and stares expressionlessly up at the ceiling. Dolly stumbles back to the wall, legs trembling, trips over a scrap of his skin and moans as she hits the wall. She cowers, sobbing loudly.

The door bursts open. Shafts of light enter the room and drift over the crimson carcass. Her father stares at it, face blank. Her mother screams.

'Daddy…' she moans.

'I know, sweetie,' he says. He's still dressed in his suit and tie, and he steps into the room, closing the door behind him. 'I'm sorry.'

'Daddy, please… please, help me. It happened again…'

'I know,' he says. His shoes are splashed with blood as he crosses the room to her and cradles her, hushing her gently. 'I know.'

***

Sheryl Stett waits outside while the two of them bundle Frank's carcass, the soiled, bloody sheets and all his skin into a tarp-lined garden sack and drag him down to the cellar. He's heavy, and Dolly struggles with her end of the bag so that his skinned head bumps the stairs on their way down. She sobs, and they take a break every few minutes. Donald comforts her, but in the same way he always does, with a soft hand on her shoulder and a gentle kiss to the forehead, and she knows he's afraid to really touch or hold her.

'Nearly there,' he says, grunting as they reach the cellar door. 'I've just gotta go get the key, wait here a sec. You okay, baby?'

Dolly nods, wiping her nose with the back of her hand. She's dressed in a pair of pyjamas but she knows they'll need to be thrown out after this; beneath, her naked skin is drenched in blood and fear and she can't bear to wear them again, not after tonight. He was nice. God, he looked at her like she was everything. And he saved her life. If that mad bastard at the tent hadn't shown up…

She listens as her dad disappears into the kitchen and rummages through the cutlery draw for the set of keys he keeps bundled up with an assortment of corkscrews and peelers. She looks down at the body in the bag. It's still open a little and she can smell him, meat and sex and blood. She can see his chest, red muscles bound to his ribs and stripped of all their skin, and she sobs into her hands, turning away.

'Here we go,' Donald says, returning with the keys. He speaks quietly, softly. Slowly, he slides the key into the lock and opens the cellar door, fumbling inside for a light switch. Fluorescent bulbs fizzle on along the wall and light a narrow, wooden staircase.

They climb down carefully, Donald first, gripping Frank's bundled legs. More lights peel on as they descend. The cellar is dank with cobwebs and dust and a manky, choking smell. They reach the bottom and drop Frank's bagged corpse onto the cement floor. Little clouds of dust kick up beneath the weighted tarpaulin.

'Bulb's out,' Donald said, nodding at the ceiling. 'Give me a sec, baby. I'm gonna go grab a torch, I can't see shit down here.'

Dolly frowns, watching as he climbs the stairs. 'I can see fine,' she calls up after him. She wishes she couldn't. Beside her, the bag shifts. 'Dad, hang on, I'll come with you.'

She starts towards the stairs as he reaches the top and steps through.

The door closes.

'Dad!' she yells.

Click.

She runs to the top of the stairs, every footstep loud and thumping in her ears. It echoes about the cellar and she reaches the door, pounds on it with both fists.

'Daddy, let me out!'

She can hear him breathing the other side of the wood. He sobs.

'Daddy, please, what are you doing? Unlock the door!'

'I'm sorry, baby,' he moans. She listens as he slides the key back into his pocket. 'I'm sorry, I had to… I had to. I am so, so sorry.'

'Dad, please, what's going on?'

'He was meant to shoot you,' her father says. 'It would have been so quick. Painless, maybe. It would have… if he hadn't fucked up… baby, I'm so sorry. I don't want to do this.'

'Daddy, please.'

She claws at the wood, fumbling with the handle.

'Please…'

Nothing.

'Daddy?' she whimpers.

He's gone.

Dolly whirls around and sinks to her rump on the stairs. She buries her head in her hands but she can feel them watching, can't keep her eyes off them for fear they'll move or shift in the dark. She looks, hardly able to stop herself.

Frank's bag lies still in the middle of the room, bathed in the damp glow of the crackling lights. She's almost grateful he's still in the sack, because it means he can't stare up at her with that crimson, eyeless face of marred muscle and flashing bone.

It's the others she's worried about.

There are dozens of them, slumped against the walls and cradling each other with skinless arms. Some of them still have their eyes in their heads and they bulge, white and wet and rotting, from the shadows. Most are boys, most her age. Some a couple of years older. All dead, all because of *her*.

The carcasses are piled high atop each other, stringy nests of blood-red muscle and narrow lengths of bone wrapped in death and sinew and translucent, fading mucus. The eldest of them have started to rot and white fur grows on the meat, spreading in shining, stale patches in the half-light.

She had thought it would be different this time.

'Daddy,' she moans, leaning her head against the wood of the locked cellar door, but he's gone, and she's alone with the skinned bodies of her victims and a flower, growing out of a crack in the concrete above her head, that looks like a tiny, red rose.

LAIR OF THE LEECH
(SHUDDERING DE'ATH: PART ONE)

He watched, through the windscreen of a battered, first-generation Ford Neon he had had since the mid-nineties, as brittle Autumn leaves fluttered drily across the empty car park. The retail estate had been abandoned for half a dozen years and most of the signs from the once-grand husks of shops around the lot had fallen away or faded, removed when the owners moved camp or splashed with graffiti in the shape of green, bulging eyeballs and little red demons with twisted, yellow horns. The buildings themselves loomed over a long stretch of cracked tarmac and threw long, square shadows over the drawn paint and gravel-strewn ground. He had passed a sign, on his way in, that said *April Leaf Retail Park,* and underneath, a faded subtitle (*Home to Ambrogio Pets, April Leaf walk-in Medical Centre, and McDonald's)* had been sprayed over with dusty purple so that it now read *Home to SHIT ALL.*

Howard could see the medical centre, halfway along the estate – he had parked right in the far corner, under the shadow of a lurching tree whose roots had spread into the tarmac and pushed it upward – and his eyes passed over it briefly, curious. He had heard something on the news about some group of doctors using the old place to test a new drug that the police had later classified as "too dangerous for public or private use", but there was no sign of movement now. The sign had been stripped away and a flower – some orchid, or something – was tacked to the front of the building like a sigil. Beside it, the shell of some long-forgotten carpet emporium, and three doors along, right in the opposite corner of the estate from where Howard was watching, *Ambrogio Pets and Aquarium.*

It was one of the only buildings to still have all its glass front, although every window had been boarded up and covered in fluttering, black tarpaulin. It wasn't a big place, not half as big as the medical centre or the electronics shop just across the car park from the Neon; just a little corner stack with a flat roof and a sign that was almost intact; the text was a faded red and there was a little graphic of a wide-eyed, gulping fish that might at one point have been blue or green.

Howard glanced toward the passenger seat and shivered. The little box (he had used the case from an old cribbage game his father had given him, because it had a silver clasp on it and it was more secure than a plastic bag) was made of a dark, crimson leather and all along one edge pointed ivory triangles curled up onto the lid. Gingerly, half-afraid to touch the thing, he took it by one corner and leaned across to pop open the glovebox, shoving the cribbage case inside and jamming it closed again.

'Alright,' he told himself, drawing in a breath. He looked up into the rearview mirror: dark eyes scowled back at him from a furrowed brow; brown (greying) hair peeled back from his temples and tangled over his forehead in rigid knots; coated in stubble, his jaw set into a grim, determined frown. 'Let's get this over with.'

Slotting the key into the ignition, Howard reached behind the driver's seat and hauled a splintered, eighteen-inch stake onto the passenger seat. It was stained black at the jagged point and rivulets of dried, dark blood ran down its length in knots and spirals. Laying a hand on it for a moment, he clutched at the necklace drawn around his throat (a silver, shining cross laid in with the initials of his mother and father) and prayed.

Howard Stone turned the key in the ignition and the engine sputtered to life. He didn't want to drag the car any closer, but he knew if it came to running he would want it close by. They were faster than him, on foot, much faster – having his broken-up little Getaway Neon six feet from the door could only be a good idea.

He shifted into first and drove almost silently across the estate, passing the electronics shop and a little D.I.Y. store next to it, trawling the entire length of the car park before pulling into a space just a little way down from *Ambrogio.* He sat for a moment, after turning the engine off and yanking up the handbrake, glancing around to make sure he wasn't being watched. The lot was empty. Behind a row of gnarled trees across from him, the main road was quiet. The sun had fallen almost completely beyond the horizon and the sky was a mess of orange bands.

Howard grabbed the stake and slid it into the inside of his jacket and, with one last look at the glovebox he opened the door and stepped out of the car.

Through glass panes in the door, a life-size plastic Alsatian watched Howard Stone step up off the tarmac and approach the decrepit little shop. He locked eyes with the thing and grimaced. There was something about its face – canine mouth pulled up into an unnatural smile, tongue hanging out and dripping flakes of pink paint, a slot right between his eyes draped in cobwebs – that made him uncomfortable. He glanced over his shoulder and moved to the lock, sliding a curled pin into the door and twisting.

He wrenched it open, grunting, peeling the stiff, plastic-framed thing out of the clutches of the face of the shop and stepping through. Darkness fell across him and he laid a hand on the plastic dog's head, looking around. The place smelled like ancient, stale pet food and shit; droppings covered the tiled floor and a low reception desk in the corner to his right was drenched in webbing and dust. Cautiously, he reached into his jacket for a torch and flicked it on, swinging the beam around.

The old shop still looked almost as it might have in its heyday, except the shelves that made two aisles down the length of the room were empty and all the frames on the walls were empty of the posters that he thought might once have said, *Adopt me: I won't bite!,* or *Ambrogio own-brand Pet Food: the best money can buy!*

He stepped forward; the torch beam cast a wide, pale circle on the walls and curled over old displays swiped clean of toys and bagged food and left to crumble; a cracked fish-tank gleamed in the torchlight, evidently too worthless to take when the owners moved shop.

'I know you're here,' Howard called. 'And I know the element of surprise is wasted on you, so you may as well show your face.'

Nothing.

At the back of the shop, a sign above a rigid opening read: *Aquarium.* Beyond long, hanging strings of beads that danced and *clack*ed together in the breeze that had followed him inside, a faint blue glow seeped out of the back room and spread cool shade over the tiles at the rear of the shop.

Howard moved forward slowly, glancing up to the

ceiling. A tiny, red light flashed at the hood of a security camera. The lens was pointed at him and the camera was clean of dust, like the batteries had been fitted recently. He knew they didn't need cameras to see him.

'Hey!' he called. 'I know you clocked me the second I stepped in the door, you blood-drinking fucker! Show your damn *face!*'

Something fluttered behind him and he whirled round, grabbing at the stake in his coat. Still fingers wrapped around the rough, wooden shaft and his eyes flitted across the doorway. Nothing moved, saved for a sprinkling of wilted leaves outside that drifted lazily past the glass. The back of the dog's head was scarred and scratched and long, pale marks ran from its neck to its rump where a faded-paint tail drooped to the model's base and curled around. Movement in the corner of his eye led Howard to turn his eyes south, to the reception counter, and he watched as a cockroach scuttled across the wood and stopped halfway, eyes on him.

'Piss off,' Howard whispered, turning back toward the aquarium and lowering his hand. The stake pressed against his chest, a cooling almost-reassurance. He took a step further and the pet shop stink grew so it was horrible and overpowering. The sounds from the back room grew, too: a faint, low gurgling that was almost constant but paused every half-minute for a few seconds; the silence left in its wake was filled with a soft, breathy whisper, the faltering cry of a decade-old

135

ventilation system.

The blue lights flickered.

Howard spun around again as a shadow flitted across the blue lights and he saw the cockroach, still. Its legs poked upward; the shell on its back had been crushed inward and thin, black gunk drizzled out onto the counter. Suddenly the plastic dog statue toppled, crashing to the floor, and Howard stepped back, exploring the shadows behind the dog as it rolled on its head, torchlight landing on…

Nothing.

'Behind you,' the thing whispered, and he turned.

A cold wave of air passed from the spot behind him and he cursed. Nothing there, again. He pressed forward, walking with a new determination, fuelled by a frustration that clouded his throat and made his blood thick and hot. 'Enough with the tricks!' he yelled. 'Face me, you coward!'

The thing moved in shadows and drifts of evaporated dog-piss, brushing those long, slender fingers over the empty shelves in the shop and laughing with some low, bitter glee that made Howard cold.

He turned one last time before stepping through into the aquarium, swinging the torch around wildly. Nothing moved; even the shadows at the edges of the room that had seconds ago writhed and twisted with such suspicious brevity were still and empty.

Howard stepped through the bead curtain, wincing

as cold plastic draped over his face and brushed his cheeks. The strings rattled over his shoulders and the blue lights became green and sickly. Once his eyes had adjusted to this new, strange light he looked around; glass cabinets, all the way around the room – no, not cabinets, but tanks, rows and rows of them stacked in vertical shafts up to the ceiling, pressed into the black walls and filled with bubbling, blue-tinted water. To his left, a single table and chair where, he imagined, someone might have sat customers down to go through whatever paperwork needed signing to buy a fish. Howard assumed there was paperwork. He had never wanted a fish.

'So you're hiding in here, huh?' he said. 'In the creepy tank room. No worries.'

He turned the torch beam to the right, saw that the wall at the far end of the aquarium was home to a single, massive floor-to-ceiling tank. A struggling shape moved behind the glass and he swallowed.

Slowly, he crossed the room, peering into one of the miniature enclosures at eye-level. The glass could only have been half an inch thick but it distorted the image of whatever insane creature was kept inside so that the thin, straggly tentacles and the whip-like body looked fat and bloated. It had a single, grape-sized eye that was black and hollow, like a shark's, a flat, shining disc of nothing that seemed almost as though it had been stapled to the creature's body; it didn't move, when the thing pressed its suckers to the glass, didn't blink or turn even once. Translucent, purple skin was lined with hair-thin veins and it bulged outwards every time the thing moved. Howard glanced down, at a paper sign tacked to the outside of the glass, a little business-card-sized thing that told him Honey and Jam, two adult goldfish, would be the perfect pets for a family.

He suspected Honey and Jam were long-dead.

'I know you're watching me,' Howard said quietly as he moved along, pausing to inspect the next tank. 'Why don't you say hi?'

A fish the size of a dinner-plate lay flat on the bottom of the tank with one wing pressed up, resting against the back wall. It peeled outward when it clocked Howard and the thing gave him a surreal almost-wave.

The next tank contained a little swarm of dot-sized fish as black as ink with beady, white eyes – the sand beneath them was covered in a mess of tiny, white balls that he could only guess were eggs. As he moved past the shoal shimmered and dipped, their movements almost hypnotic. The next, a fairly normal-looking fish that had died but, instead of sinking and laying still in the sand, had floated up to the top of the water and hung there, belly bloated and swollen, only moving when the stream of bubbles from a filter tube pressing upwards into the water pushed it away. Beyond that, a longer tank contained two catfish-looking creatures that had spines along their backs and long, spayed fins that looked like claws. They fought, headbutting and slashing at each other with wide, fat mouths filled with barbed teeth, and Howard turned, looking all around the dim little room. His eyes met the pleading face of the thing behind the glass wall and he gulped.

'Come on,' he said. 'Don't make me wait in this shithole any longer, just come out. You know why I'm here. Are you really gonna make me look through your whole... weird experiment-fish collection before you show your ugly face?'

The torch was struck from his hand and clattered to the ground. Without thinking Howard grabbed the stake from his coat and plunged it upward; the point nailed soft flesh and dug in and he twisted, grunting as long, shadowy fingers pressed down on his face and pushed him back. He let go of the stake and it fell, drawing thick blood with it.

'Shot.'

The voice was cold and rasping and it echoed in the dark of the aquarium and Howard bent down to pick up the stake, moving fast, on instinct. It was faster, and it grabbed his wrist, twisted. He screamed as something snapped. Another hand twisted into his hair and slammed his face down into the tiles – he tasted blood, felt his nose *crunch* between his eyes and then the thing yanked his head up again and brought it crashing back down and he passed out, all at once, in a haze of dull black that swallowed him in less than a second.

Then cool fingers grabbed his throat and he blinked himself awake, snapping upward and thrusting up a fist. It caught his attacker in the chin and the thing hissed, reeling backward, then the sifting wave of unconsciousness caught Howard again and he toppled.

The floor hit him and the blue lights faded to black.

Howard woke up to find himself sitting at the table, right hand in his lap – the other, broken, dangled at his side and when he tried to lift it up the bones glanced together and sharp bolts of pain jolted up into his arm, causing him to grit his teeth and draw in a painful mess of a breath.

'Sleeping beauty rises,' the thing rasped.

Howard looked up. Behind him, blue lights blinked and swam and they threw twisting shapes over the table, blocked only by his own fluttering shadow on the wood. He shifted in his chair, wincing at a pain in his back. His hand moved slowly to the back of his head and he found a lump, half-hidden by matted tangles of hair. His nose stung. There was still blood in his mouth and he turned his head, spitting onto the floor.

The thing sat across from him, feet up on the table. Its shoes were long and black and pointed, a size eleven or twelve with soles that shone a dull grey in the weird glow of the aquarium. It wore black – Howard couldn't begin to describe the clothes, because they all melted together in one shapeless, shadowy cloak that drifted over the thing's all-at-once slender and massive frame. Its arms were folded across a broad chest and dark-skinned hands broke into long, flayed claws.

'Hello, gorgeous,' Howard grunted. He feigned a frown. 'I thought you lot were supposed to be all pale and sickly. What happened to that?'

The thing screwed up its nose. 'Is that a race comment? Really?'

Howard grinned. 'Fuck you.'

The thing moved quickly, suddenly, legs reeling and fetching back into the shadows to slide a flat, brown envelope across the table.

'What's this?' Howard said. The thing shrugged.

He opened it carefully, one-handed. There was no familiar press against his chest – the stake was gone, hidden away somewhere. Never mind that, he thought. He had contingencies. Slowly, he tipped the envelope on its end and let the contents fall out before him. Six photographs, six polaroid snaps in white, square frames. The thing reached forward and, with hands that moved like dark, flitting bursts of lightning, spread the photographs and slapped the table.

'Recognise them?' it said.

Howard nodded.

'Nothing to say?'

'No.'

The thing snarled.

They were all men, all the faces in the photographs:

an elderly man with a withered face and wispy hair; two young Peruvians with dark clothes and bloodshot eyes that looked wide and red-ringed even in the black and white images; a middle-aged man with a tweed jacket who, if not for the scarred face and the pale skin, would have looked like a geography teacher; a fisherman; a cave hermit.

They were all dead. The photographs had been taken shortly after Howard had visited them, and each one had a ruptured hole in its chest – the old man was slumped over an office chair, the fisherman curled back against the wall of an isolated log cabin with blood pooling over his shirt.

'These were my brothers,' the thing said. 'All of them.'

Howard said nothing.

They were never women; that was how they spawned, by impregnating human women, planting their wretched seed in the host and slaughtering the husk of the girl when she gave birth. The old stories about them biting humans to turn them were bollocks; if you got bit, Howard knew, that was the end. You either died full or empty, depending on how good you tasted. He had seen the shells of people fed upon. Their skin turned purple, dark, and crusted up so that it pressed against their bones and solidified. They were like insects, withered and encased in a dry, shining membrane that had once been full of colour.

'You know who I am, then,' the thing said.

'I know what you call yourself,' Howard said. 'That's why I'm here.'

'That's my name.'

'It is *not.*'

The thing's lips peeled back and Howard caught sight of its teeth, long, dark spines that poked out of slender gums and crashed against each other, all different lengths and mashed together in a mouth that opened wider and wider until the cheeks billowed out and even they were lined with rows of tiny, white points. Howard had never let one get close enough to see its mouth fully open, but he imagined it would be like a circle of white spines in a mess of red with the tonsils at the back, waiting and hungry.

'You killed them,' the thing spat, leaning forward so that the shadows curled around its dark face peeled onto the table. 'My family.'

'I've killed so many of your brothers,' Howard whispered, 'I've lost count. You think this is it?'

'Oh, no,' the thing smiled. Spines flashed blue in the dark. 'I know who your *first* was. The one, the only…'

'He's dead,' Howard grunted. 'Move on. Why haven't you killed me?'

'Oh, Mr. Stone,' the thing said, pulling an expression that was almost a perfect impression of hurt. 'You think so little of me.'

'All of you. How about you tell me your real name?'

'You *know* my real name.'

'I absolutely refuse to believe that's real. Tell me, what is it really?'

'*Phobos De'Ath,*' said the thing.

'I bet it's Geoff, or Larry, or –'

'De'Ath.'

'Shut up. Your name is *never* "Phobos Death".'

'*De'Ath,*' the thing insisted. 'Day-Ath.'

'Dee-Ath.'

'Day-Ath.'

'Day-Ath.'

'*Day*-Ath.'

'I bet it's Herbert.'

'Enough,' the thing hissed, and its eyes flared.

Howard groaned. 'Do you have any painkillers? If you're gonna make me sit here and take lessons on pronunciation, you could at least give me something for this hand.'

'You come here to kill me, and you make jokes when I take your only weapon and break you.'

'Takes a lot more than a fractured wrist to break me,' Howard said quietly.

'I wonder,' the thing said. Its lips curled up in a scarred, raw smile. 'I suppose you've been through rather a lot, haven't you? Ever since that night, back when you were just a scared, little seven-year-old. What

144

was her name again?'

'Don't you dare.'

'So monster-hunters have sore spots too,' De'Ath whispered.

Howard stood up, suddenly, turning his head. 'What is this place?' he said. 'Oh, don't get up. You could have your hands round my throat before I make it halfway out this room, what do you think I'm gonna do? Try and run?'

He turned, walking with his broken wrist hanging limp by his side, moving past the tanks he had already explored and bending down to peer into one at floor-level with five or six fish inside; each one had glimmering, blood-red scales and a third eye on the top of its head that swivelled with the others.

'I mean, did you make these?' Howard said, walking along toward the back of the room. 'I'm no expert but these are *weird,* right? What are they, did you cook them up in some messed-up monster lab? Or find them somewhere?'

In another tank, halfway along the wall, a starfish clutched at the glass with barbed, black claws that lined its limbs and glared up at him with an eyeless face in its belly. Its mouth opened, a pale slit in a fleshy mask of nothing, and its teeth shivered. Howard crossed the room and looked in a tank on the other side; the creature in here was pale and it zipped from one side of its little glass enclosure to the other, darting about with

145

something bloody and shrivelled in its teeth.

'The ocean is a fascinating thing,' the monster sitting at the table said. 'So vast and dark and unexplored. You know, we know less about the contents of our seas than we do about the surface of the moon.'

Howard squinted through the glass, frowning. The thing's tail was a shredded mess of red and white and crimson trails of mist seemed to sprout from it and rise into the water. The thing in its mouth twitched.

It had ripped off its own tail in some rabid hunger and it chewed, as he watched, never blinking or looking away from him even as it flitted about in its torrid frenzy.

'I am assuming you brought it with you?' De'Ath said.

Howard froze. Immediately, his thoughts shifted to the box in his car, the little cribbage case that he'd shoved into the glovebox. 'I don't know what you mean,' he said.

'You don't seem the type to ever leave home without it.'

'Not a clue what you're talking about. You're delusional, Herbert.'

'You're a fool. To come here with intent to kill me, well, that was foolish in itself. But to bring *it* with you…'

Howard turned, narrowing his eyes. 'I didn't bring

it,' he lied.

The thing smiled. Phobos De'Ath was an imposing figure, close-up, but he seemed even bigger farther away; the black cloths and rags pinned to his chest should have dragged him into the shadows but he seemed to stand out from them, commanding them, brown skin blotched and blotted with ink-spatter marks like blood and peeling flesh, eyes wet and bloodshot, bald with pointed features and lips too soft and narrow to contain what was inside without being torn apart.

'Why don't you take a look?' De'Ath said, nodding toward the back of the room. 'I know you want to, really. You may as well, before I kill you.'

Howard looked. The shape behind the clear, misted wall of the glass tank at the back of the room looked back at him. 'Is it real?' he said softly.

'Decide for yourself.'

Howard walked slowly, ignoring the flitting shapes in the tanks at his side and the bubbling and whispering of the water. Absent-mindedly, he reached for the crucifix around his neck and found it missing.

There was a stool, in front of the glass, a low, metal thing taken from the shop front, and Howard imagined the monster liked to sit here and gaze upon his abomination on the long, lonely days when nobody came to try and kill him. The glass itself was dusty and it distorted the world beyond worse than any of the others. The water whirled and bubbled around the thing

147

inside, frenzied so manically that great, white strings of bubbles rose from tubes along the bottom of the tank and crashed into a thin wash at the top. As he neared, the creature slammed its body against the glass, webbed hands spread and flattened.

'It knows I'm here,' Howard whispered.

The thing was the height of a man, but it was shaped all wrong. Its hands and feet were long and clawed and thin sheets of dark, veiny flesh joined slender fingers and toes so that when it hammered on the glass they slapped it loudly. Its movements were sluggish, slowed down by the water and drowsy, heavy. Gills carved out of its throat and shoulders fluttered. Its back was arched and spines cracked out of a curled, protruding backbone, long, feathered spikes that drifted and shivered against its skin. Its belly was caved in and torn out and its hips broke out in sharp, bony points. Its arms and legs were impossibly long and thin and Howard could make out the shapes of its bones beneath its dark, green skin.

Its face was a nightmare of bulging, black eyes ringed with fleshy circles of grey and white and deep slits where its nose should be. It was bald, as bald as Phobos De'Ath, except its head was ridged with little spikes and its mouth was not filled with long, mismatched spines but tiny, pointed stumps of grey. A long, purple tongue snaked out from its lips and curled down its chin and its jaw shifted up and down in the murk, like it was trying to say something.

'So,' De'Ath said, right behind him.

Howard jolted, turning, reaching for the stake in his jacket that wasn't there.

'Oh, I love it,' the monster whispered, leaning close enough that Howard could smell its breath. It smelled like blood and fish and pet food. 'The fear. Go on, Mr. Stone. Piss yourself. For me.'

The monster licked its lips, thin, grey tongue slithering between long teeth and curling back in with a *flit*.

'Where is it?' De'Ath said, eyes flashing with hunger. 'I looked in your coat, but it wasn't there. Did you hide it in that putrid little car of yours?'

'I'm going to kill you,' Howard whispered. Slowly, with his one good hand, he reached down and curled his fingers around the rim of the stool.

'I bet that's exactly where it is,' De'Ath said. 'Perfect.'

'You want it?'

'Oh, you know that I do.'

'Go get it, bitch,' Howard hissed, and he lifted the stool and slammed it into the glass behind him.

The stool bounced off with a *thwunk* and his good arm winced.

Howard turned, looked up. The impact had barely made a scratch. In the water, the helpless creature had reeled back but it returned, now, to the glass and slapped

149

with its webbed hands frantically, desperately.

'Six inches thick,' De'Ath said. 'You're a fucking idiot.'

Howard dropped the stool and took a step back. 'Shit.'

De'Ath bore down on him, arms outstretched, claws shearing trails out of the blue-tinted air. Black trailed off him and engulfed the light and Howard shook his head, raising his good hand in front of his face.

'No,' De'Ath said, grabbing Howard's fingers and tearing them downward. Something in the man's arm popped. '*Look.*'

He looked.

There were more of them in the shadows; no, they *were* the shadows, great towers of shade in all the green and blue and black. They hissed, a dozen of them – two dozen, rearing up from the darkness and clawing at the air. Every one of them looked less human than the last so that the worst, the most monstrous, was just a mask of pale, scarred flesh with two blood-filled eyes and a hissing mouth, all wrapped in black and swiping madly at its own face. Another lurched forward and snapped its teeth right in Howard's ear, brushing his cheek with long, bony claws ridged with scars and gouges.

'No,' Howard whispered, pressing himself into the corner of the room. Behind him, the thing pounded on the walls of its glass prison but its movements were too slow, dragged down by the water. Outside, past the front of the shop, he heard glass shatter and he knew they'd got into his car.

'It's ours,' De'Ath hissed, and he swept forward and grabbed Howard by the throat. The monster smiled, inches from his face, and said, '*Fool,*' and then they were upon him, biting and scratching and clawing at his skin, and all he could do was scream and scramble at the dark as his own blood seeped over his flesh and his mouth filled up with it and their bony, knotted hands dragged him into the shadows and began to tear at his meat.

Howard was sprawled on his belly on the floor. It was a different floor, a concrete floor, and when he tried to move he found his whole left arm hurt so badly it must have been broken, and his jacket had been shredded; looking down, he saw that ribbons of skin had been peeled off his torso and patched up, badly, with bandage and gauze.

His blood would taste better, when the fear had drained out of his system and been replaced by pain and dull, numb acceptance. Slowly, with his good hand – which now was a mess of slick, raw muscle and bone, with one finger torn off altogether and his thumb bent backwards – he reached for his face. His skin was rough and thin, but not fully dehydrated. He could still feel his pulse, although it was weak and sombre.

He rolled onto his back, screaming.

It watched him from the shadows, pale-skinned and slumped against a cement wall.

'What are you?' he whispered. Dark shapes swam in front of him. It wasn't one of them. It wasn't human, either. As he listened, he heard it breathing in the shadows, and its breaths were long and shallow. *H-h-h-h-h-huhhh*...

His eyes flitted left and right and he saw that the room was filled with scraps, flesh and scales and clothes but not a drop of blood, no, they wouldn't waste it. He saw bones littered along one side of the room, rotting carcasses of fish and odd, squid-looking creatures spread loosely over them. Deflated and hollow. Husks.

The creature stood.

'No,' Howard whispered. 'Please...'

H-h-h-huhhh...

He tried to sit up but the peeled flesh of his hips stung and burned and he howled. He could hear them upstairs, poring over the ceiling with soft-footed steps. Dozens of them. More than he had ever seen. Even in the nest he'd stumbled on in Peru there had only been five of the things. He had gutted them all.

'Please, whatever you are, don't...' Howard whispered. He gasped for air, suddenly aware that his throat was rammed with dust and flecks of his own skin.

The thing stepped closer, dragging long, flat feet over the concrete.

'Do it,' Howard whispered. 'Kill me.'

It stood over him and its mouth opened. A long, slow string of drool peeled over a white, fleshy bottom lip and met Howard's face, wet and sticky.

'Please,' he said. He closed his eyes as the thing leant down, pink and white and choking on its own throat.

H-h-h-h-h-huhhh…

WENDIGO WEEPING
(SHUDDERING DE'ATH: PART TWO)

The boy laid awake, eyes closed, pretending with every fibre in him to be asleep as he listened to the footsteps in the hall. It was gone midnight and he couldn't remember ever staying up so late. Not since last Christmas, anyway.

The footsteps stopped for a second and he blinked one eye open, glancing toward his door from the bed in the corner of the room. He had left it open, just a little, so that as soon as the shuffling figure of Santa Claus threw a shadow across the gap he would know to screw his eyes shut again and keep quiet. Orange light seeped in from the landing and he waited. *One, two, three...*

The footsteps resumed and he smiled a little, grinning mouth pushing round cheeks out into the soft surroundings of the duvet he'd pulled tight to his throat. He was still in his clothes.

He counted three long, shambling steps before the Christmas Eve visitor stopped at Carrie's door. She had the room just down the hall, by the stairs; it only made sense that Santa would visit her first, having come from the fireplace in the living room and traipsed up with his sack full of toys. She had a pillowcase hung on the doorhandle, on the inside of her room (their parents had told them to leave the pillowcases *outside,* but of course then they would never have even the slightest chance of seeing Father Christmas and where was the fun in that?) and Howard listened as the door squealed open on old, rusted hinges.

He heard heavy, coarse breathing and after a moment the footsteps resumed as Santa walked right past his sister's pillowcase and crossed the room to her bed.

Howard heard a scream.

He snapped awake and tore the sheets off, stumbling out of bed and almost tripping over his feet. Maybe Carrie had forgotten it was Christmas Eve and been awoken by the long, juddering sounds of Santa's footsteps only to look right up into his face – it was surprise, that was all. A long, harrowing shriek of surprise.

Or maybe Santa Claus wasn't really Santa Claus.

Howard lurched into the hallway, squinting as the bright lights thrust into his eyes. Her door was wide open and he staggered toward it, legs half-working and half set in some sleepy wet-cement state. The visitor had dragged up the carpet in long, scarred tufts where it had dragged its heels and Howard stumbled around the open doorframe and froze.

Even in the dark, he could see that it wasn't Santa Claus.

'Hey!' Howard yelled, but it didn't turn towards him. It was leant over his sister's body, one hand curled beneath her neck to support her head. Her eyes had rolled back in her skull and her hair fell away from her face as the shadow pressed its mouth to her neck and bit.

Howard couldn't move. He tried, but something froze him there, paralysed him so that he couldn't speak or scream or tumble forward; all he could do was watch as a thick, lumpy tube shot out of the thing's mouth and punctured the skin of Carrie's neck. It reeled back and a cluster of tiny, egg-like sacs fell into the open, bleeding wound and melted into her flesh, dissolving in all the red and flowing streams of crimson.

The shadow turned, tongue whipping back into its mouth, and seven-year-old Howard Stone caught a glimpse of its teeth, long slivers of bone that jutted this way and that from blood-spattered gums. Its eyes flashed a bright, piercing yellow and suddenly it was six inches from his face and breathing right into his mouth. Its skin was pale and stricken with thin, bloody veins that pulsed and wriggled; its hair was black and thin and hung off a peeling scalp in patches and clumps that had been dragged back toward a thin, fleshy neck. It was dressed all in black.

It grinned. Pointed teeth flared white inside its

cheeks. 'Shh,' it said, and then it flitted back to the bed and wrapped its arms around his sister's body and lifted her up.

'No!' Howard yelled, taking a step forward. Immediately the thing moved, dropping his sister to the floor with a *crack!* and it towered over him, a shadow that filled up the whole room as it raised its clawed hands and swiped at him. Howard ducked, but the thing was faster than him and it plunged a hand into his belly, forcing him against the wall. His head smacked the plaster and he slid down to the floor, groaning. Already the shadow had returned to Carrie's limp body and it picked her up easily, like she was weightless.

The thing moved to the bedroom window and cracked it open with one clawed hand, hauling the girl over his shoulder. Howard knew that it could never fit out of the frame, but in moments it was gone.

He stood, head pounding, stumbling to the window. He looked down and saw a shadow writhe across the driveway and disappear into the dark, and then his sister was gone.

'Mum!' he yelled. 'Mum! Dad!'

He turned, hobbling past the empty pillowcase on Carrie's door and lunging down the stairs. He found them in the living room, spread across the carpet; his father was a husk of dry, grey skin and brittle, snapped bones, bent-up and tossed against the radiator so that his hair crackled in the heat and his eyes, wide open and

157

clouded with blood, rolled outwards. He was a shell of grey an brown all dressed in red-and-blue striped pyjamas and splashed with blood that had been lapped up by a horrible, flat tongue.

Howard's mother was still alive, but the shadow had torn off her legs and her body ended in two bloody stumps that spilled red onto the carpet. Her bones flashed white in the crackling light from the fireplace. Everything smelled of *red*.

'Mum…' Howard sobbed, kneeling over her.

'Where is she?' his mother croaked. She grabbed his hand, tried to squeeze it, but her fingers were weak and she slipped. 'Did he take her?'

Howard nodded. 'I'm sorry. I tried to stop him. I…'

'It's okay,' his mother said, smiling weakly. 'I need you to find her, Howie. Can you do that for me? Can you find her again?'

He nodded.

She coughed, and blood-red bubbles trailed over her lips. 'Your Christmas presents… are in the cupboard in our bedroom. Howie, *find* her. Please.'

Then she was gone.

Howard tried to follow the shadow out into the night, but he was a child, and he was exhausted and distraught and his legs would only carry him so far into the shadows before he realised he was chasing at nothing. He yelled her name into the street, but the only response he got was the shutting off of all the lights in the

Johnson place.

Orphaned, terrified, Howard Stone went home and, with nothing else to do except find out what had taken his sister, he went into his parents' bedroom and unwrapped his presents with a slow, sorrowful callousness. His mother had given him a silver cross on a chain; his father, a red, leather cribbage case.

The creature was an abomination, an eight-foot mountain of sick flesh soldered to thick, muscular arms and legs; its skin was pure white but bruised a deep, rosy pink in curls around its abdomen and a faint purple across its groin and throat; its hands were webbed, like the hands of the thing in the tank, but there were no gills, and its whole body was stiff and dry with rigor mortis. It had the skin of a corpse but it was all plastered on wrong, like the body beneath belonged to something else. Its face was completely featureless, and without a nose or mouth Howard wondered where that dreadful, ragged breathing was coming from, and then he saw the slits cut across its ribs that fluttered and shook with every long exhalation and realised they were gills.

The thing leant down and grabbed him by the throat, strong fingers crashing around his windpipe and squeezing. It picked him up, some inhuman strength allowing it to lift him almost entirely off the floor with a single hand, and before he could protest or grapple with the abomination's wrist it had tossed him against a clanging, metal wall and let him fall so that he was sitting.

Howard gasped, clutching at a torn-up belly with his broken hand. The fear coursed through him so thick and hot and agonising that the pain almost faded into one numb blanket of needles that dug into his skin and left him unfeeling. He looked up through swollen eyelids and saw that the creature had paused, head tilted, towering above him but not attacking or clawing at him, just watching.

He looked up into its face and saw that a set of long, jagged scars had been dragged from the top of its scalp to the smooth nothing where its mouth would have been. There were more, all over; there was not a speck of blood or red on the thing, and every scar had dried and crusted over so cleanly that they were almost invisible, but its whole living carcass was lined with them.

'What are you?' Howard said. He looked over his shoulder – the wall behind his head was not a wall at all but a stacked row of lockers, green doors peeling and hanging open. The concrete floor was torn up in places and patched over where more lockers or benches had been ripped out. The creature watched him with a fleshy, eyeless curiosity and Howard shifted his gaze back to the thing, wary of leaving it unseen for too long. 'Can you speak? Can you understand me?'

The thing took a step back and slumped against the

opposite wall. Bones tumbled away from its thighs as its rump hit the floor and it reached for a half-eaten fish corpse laid by its feet. Long, white fingers drifted around the scaled body of the thing and raised it to a face without a mouth.

'I know what you are,' Howard whispered.

Without warning, the abomination's face wrenched open and a wide, red mouth burst forth, teeth snapping and white and terrible, stained orange with blood and sheltering a long, fat, red tongue. The gaping maw sucked in the fish carcass and closed on itself, leaving hardly a mark on the creature's pale, featureless face. Howard listened to it chew. The sounds were wet and sloppy but muffled through the layer of skin that had clamped itself over the abomination's mouth and fused together.

He had seen the corpse of a creature like this in Peru, hung outside the nest by its neck. The gills across its ribs had been stuffed with clay and a stake had been driven through its chest, another through its belly, all the way through so that its insides drizzled down the back of its legs. The villagers had called it *Vampiro Albino*. He had called it a white leech. It was one of them, but, like a failed experiment, they detested it, shunned it.

'Can you help me?' Howard said quietly. He tried to sit up straight, but his torso threatened to explode outward if he strained the raw skin any further, so he stayed slumped and watched as the thing swallowed and turned its head back towards him. 'Hey, Whitey. Raise one finger if you know what I'm saying.'

The abomination didn't move.

'One finger. If you can understand me. Please.'

Nothing. Slowly, the creature leant across to grab another carcass, a still, thin-bodied fish with the scales half-dragged off its body so the raw, pink mess beneath glistened through. Howard watched as the abomination's face opened, flesh tearing apart to reveal that horrible crashing mess of a mouth, watched as the fish slithered between its teeth and disappeared down its throat, watched as the skin sealed up again and the creature leant its head back against the wall.

'Fine,' Howard said. He laid his better hand – the one with the peeled skin and the missing finger, the one that hurt like *shit* whenever he moved it – on the ragged mess of his torso and stood, slowly, gritting his teeth all the while so he didn't bite his tongue. Halfway up the wall he grunted, stopping to pant and to slap his broken wrist uselessly against a leg that seemed to have given up on him. Pain jolted all the way up his arm and he resisted the powerful urge to screech into the dark. 'I'll just go,' he rasped, 'without you.'

His eyes landed on the abomination's face and he saw that it was watching him again, blank and still but fixed on him.

'What?' he spat. '*What,* Whitey? They've got it – the

box. I can't let them…'

Slowly, the creature lifted a finger.

'Unbelievable,' Howard breathed.

The finger curled into a crooked, white claw and pointed into a corner of the room over Howard's left shoulder. He turned his head, following the direction of the creature's slender digit until he saw it, a set of concrete steps leading upward. There was a green *EXIT* sign on the wall that had long-since lost its glow and cracked right from the middle.

Howard almost smiled. He started to move, dragging himself across the swinging locker doors with a loud clatter. His legs worked, almost perfectly, and he found that focusing on the stink of fish and death helped him to ignore the pain in his arms and gut enough to reach the bottom of the stairs, slumping forward and crashing to his knees on the concrete in one panting mess of exhaustion.

He turned. 'Are you coming?' he groaned, voice cracking as his throat burned with a cool, shearing pain.

The abomination stood, slowly, arms hanging by its sides. Slowly, its face tore open with a loud *shuuk* and its red maw of a mouth curled into a smile, spiny teeth locked together. Fish scales danced and glittered on its gums.

'*Hungry…*' it whispered, and it started to follow him up the stairs.

The police found her a year later, stuffed into a bag laced with rocks and dumped into the Tyne. They opened the bag on the banks of the river and she tumbled out, belly carved open with a knife that had split her flesh in rough, jagged sheets. The case made the news: *Pregnant Child Found Dead, Identity Unknown.* They did not disclose her age, and the photographs were "too graphic and disturbing" to be released publicly, but Howard knew it was her. He was eight years old now and he knew what they were, these awful creatures that stole women and children from their homes and made hosts of them, discarded their carcasses when they had spawned some unnatural monster-child and went looking for more unwilling surrogates.

He had found one of them already.

Two streets across from the orphanage, a man's wife went missing. Her name was Nancy Barker. She was thirty-two years old and she had blonde hair and striking, green eyes. Her husband described the kidnapper as some seven-and-a-half feet tall, dressed in a black suit and tie with pale skin and a beard that was all wispy, black hair. He said the man was bald and his head shone like it was wet with mucus.

Howard waited. He knew, even then, four years off pubescence and another six or seven till adulthood, that the longer he waited the more would die. But he had to be *sure.* Over the next two weeks, six more women were taken from the area, and he plotted them out in red marker on an Ordnance Survey map he kept folded under his pillow. In the middle of all the red crosses and scrawled lines was an abandoned slaughterhouse: *Straub & Sons' Fine Meat Abattoir.* Straub had killed himself in an office in the building – his sons had found him with a gun in his hand, the bullet having crashed through his brain and the security glass window behind his head, leaving a sloppy trail of pink and red spattered over the office chair and the wall – and the abattoir had closed down. A week later, the kidnappings begun.

Howard went, one night, sneaking out of the back door of the orphanage and leaving it open just a crack so that he could get back in unnoticed. The abattoir was a twelve-minute walk and he packed a bottle of water that he'd conducted some semblance of a prayer over (in the vague hopes that this was how Holy Water was produced, and the even less certain hopes that it would be enough to wound a creature like the one he was facing) and a stake he'd fashioned out of half a fencepost. He wore his mother's cross around his neck. He had read, somewhere, that it would protect him.

After he had carved a point on the stake fine enough to puncture skin, he scratched two sets of initials into the cross with the very tip of the knife blade.

They would be proud of him.

***

The sounds of faint, low chanting grew louder as he neared the top of the stairs, half-slumped on one rail with his hands dangling, almost useless by his sides. The creatures spoke with one rasping, thrumming voice that seemed to spread across the floor beneath Howard's feet and ring about the plaster in the walls, vibrating and pulsing – like the buzz of a crowd at a football stadium, but harsh and horrific. There were words, amongst the throbbing and beneath the pounding of his tired heart, but they weren't English, or any language he recognised; some old, dead language that long preceded any he knew at all.

The language of the leech.

He turned, when he reached the top of the stairs, elbow laid against a bar across the door. It wasn't locked. Well, he supposed, he had no reason to come out of the nice safe cellar-cum-locker-room with the albino vampire and the dead fish, only to burst into a room full of dead lights and cruel-lipped monsters. He wasn't an idiot.

'Ready, Whitey?'

The abomination said nothing. Its face had sealed up again and he could see the faint silhouettes of its teeth behind the fused, thin flesh of its maw, bony and pressing against it like the bones in its slim fingers. Its breathing echoed in some strange, hypnotic rhythm with the chanting past the door: *H-h-huuhhhh-h-huh*...

Halfway up the stairs, its head was bent forward,

neck craned, swaying arms hanging so low that its narrow claws brushed the ground. The gills scraped out of its chest fluttered in harmony and low, weeping sounds seemed to filter out of them.

Howard turned and glanced down at the bar. There would be no element of surprise, no moment of advantageous mystery. In less than a second they would be on him, and he would have to run and hope that Whitey was human enough, and enraged enough at the less deformed members of its sick species that had imprisoned it, to fight them off for him.

He pushed open the door. It squealed.

Shadows lurched up onto the walls and swarmed the glass tanks, swallowing blue light as they danced and swam in the glow. The creatures were gathered in a ring in the centre of the aquarium, and those who weren't a part of the intertwined, writhing inner circle pushed from the outside to get in, shoving and thrusting and hissing with bared, blood-stained teeth. Howard watched, staring as they moved in one black-and-white mess of pale skin and dark clothes and long, shining nails that glistened with mucus, surrounding the dark-skinned Phobos De'Ath as he led their haunting chant.

He was holding the cribbage case.

He raised it high, locking eyes with Howard and winking. 'Visitors!' the creature yelled, voice just as piercing and awful as before. His gleeful cry did not interrupt the chanting; all the while they grew louder, some murmuring through gritted, spiny teeth, others slobbering the words over wet, flitting tongues. 'Brothers, the man of the hour has returned to bear witness!'

De'Ath's gaze shifted to the abomination and he smiled, almost sadly, rapping his claws on the rim of the leather box.

'And he's brought our dear friend, the damned fish-eater, the *wendigo!*'

One of the creatures snapped its teeth and writhed, shoulders knotting in a whirl of black as it darted from the circle and lunged towards Howard and the albino vampire. De'Ath snapped his fingers and another blur crashed out of the ring, tackling the first and burying its teeth in the mutineer's neck. Black, ink-like blood spurted as the second creature dragged a great chunk of flesh out of the first's throat and chewed, spitting gobs of white and purple everywhere in a wide, spiralling spray of spittle.

'Brilliant,' De'Ath whispered.

'What are you doing?' Howard yelled. 'You can't open that!'

Long, delicate fingers toyed with the clasp and De'Ath's mouth opened enough that Howard could see the creature's tongue playing around the serrated edges of those long, shrill teeth and he stumbled forward, whole body trembling with pain, shaking his head.

'Please,' he moaned, 'please, don't open that box.'

168

A filthy, cracked claw dusted with wet clumps of red and brown slid under the clasp and flicked it up with a *click*.

'Please!' Howard screamed. He pushed into the circle and long, rough hands grabbed his arms and his shoulders and tugged him back, pinning him by the throat to the wall. Behind him, black fish danced behind the glass and screamed into the water. 'Please, don't do this!'

Whitey had taken a step into the room but the abomination was distracted, focused on the thing in the ceiling-height tank at the back of the room. It stared blindly into the mist beyond the six-inch glass and the thing inside stared back.

'Help me,' Howard croaked. Claws pressed into the flesh beneath his chin and held him there, helpless.

De'Ath opened the box.

The heart spilled out in a sifting torrent of sand and salt, landing on the hard floor with a soft, wet *splat*. The creature grinned, tossing the box into the snarling mob behind him and leaning down to scoop the organ off the floor. The heart was still, purple and red and wet, a thin coat of muscle ground in with salt like a seasoned chicken breast, still slick from being pulled straight out of the bird's carcass. The arteries poking out of the thing had been severed so the pale ends of flapping, rubbery tubes were all that remained.

De'Ath raised the heart to his nose and sniffed.

'It's time,' he breathed. 'Bring him!'

Bony claws yanked Howard by the hair and his broken arm and thrust him into the circle. De'Ath gripped Howard by the throat and turned his head down so that he was staring right at it: at the purple, dead heart in the creature's clawed hand.

'You know what I need,' the vampire murmured, lips so close to Howard's ear he could feel the blood wafting over his cheek. The voice was low and soft and almost seductive. 'Will you give it to me?'

'There's enough of it on me,' Howard grunted, struggling against the creature's grip. Spittle flew from his gritted teeth. 'Take it.'

De'Ath looked him over and smiled, eyes narrowing to fine, flashing points that shone a wet, deathly blue in the light from the aquarium walls. 'Better to take it fresh,' he hissed, and he slid the tip of a long, jagged claw across Howard's throat.

Howard tried to scream as the agony seared his neck and burned his face and a warmth spread and drizzled down to his chest, but the scream came out as a gurgle and already De'Ath had taken his bloody claw and drawn a symbol into the heart in glistening, wet red. A smiley face: two little dots for the eyes and a crooked, crimson mouth.

'And with that,' De'Ath cried, raising the heart high and squeezing it so that beads of blood ran through his fingers, 'with the heart of the dead and the blood of the bastard who killed him, our brother is *reborn!*'

The snarling and chanting turned to a frenzied, rabid shriek of hunger that rattled in their throats as they swiped at the heart with manic claws and snapped at the air with their ringed maws. They looked like hookworms, pale bodies crowned with a circle of red-raw gums and teeth so they could latch on to flesh and suck the life from it. Blood foamed at the mouth of one and it scrambled into the circle, scratching at its brothers in some insane try at reaching the heart.

Nothing happened.

De'Ath glanced down at Howard, grip loosening a little. The creature's face was marred, just for a fraction of a second, by what looked like a frown.

'Nice try,' Howard gurgled. The slit in his throat wasn't deep, but the blood was still fanning from it and spilling down him.

'More blood, then,' De'Ath hissed, and he raised a curled, black claw to Howard's eye. The point pressed against the man's iris and drew a tear and he snarled.

'Or a different heart,' Howard suggested, voice hoarse with agony.

De'Ath hesitated.

'Try it again. Who knows, maybe your father – that is who I killed, back at the abattoir, isn't it? You were born out of one of the women he kidnapped? – maybe he'll be *reborn* if you just try the whole ritual again.'

'Quiet,' De'Ath hissed.

'Maybe he'll come back if you take more blood,' Howard grunted. 'Maybe if you take some more out of me and draw a nice little flower in all that useless meat, he'll come back.'

De'Ath sniffed the heart again.

'Or maybe it's the *wrong heart.*'

Suddenly De'Ath dropped him and Howard screamed as his fractured bones smacked the ground. The creature lifted the heart to its mouth and opened wide, long teeth shooting out of its gums and puncturing the muscle, shredding it open so that strings of long-dried blood spat out of the thing.

'Human!' De'Ath snarled. 'He *tricked* us with a human heart.'

'Yeah,' Howard groaned, clutching at his belly, 'just don't ask where it came from.'

De'Ath looked around, at the snarling mob of vampires clutching and clawing at the bleeding heart in his hand, and then his eyes fell on Howard and he pointed a curled claw at the man's face. Whispering so softly Howard could barely hear, he said, 'Kill him,' and the creatures descended in a thrashing wave of darkness.

The abattoir was a maze of steel-lined corridors and wide, open spaces that had been stripped of all their gruesome machinery; it was empty, but eight-year-old Howard Stone could smell the death on the walls. He found the nest in the very bowels of the building, a metal door at the end of a corridor lit with deep, red emergency bulbs that opened with the slightest push. And beyond it, a room stuffed with nightmares.

The floor was a mess of bones and teeth and hard, brittle skins that looked like they'd been peeled right off their bodies. Scraps of tangled, matted hair were packed around the walls of the room amongst the bodies of drained, thin cows; all their meat had been taken, the blood flushed from their veins so that the cracking skin fell over angular ribs and sagged about caved bellies and withering skulls. Howard recognised one of the Straub sons, his carcass strung up from the ceiling by a meathook, from a picture in the newspaper, although his face was gaunt and eyeless and his hair was as flayed as his knotted, curled fingers. The meathook had been stabbed through his dehydrated shoulder and there was no blood. The whole place stank of it, but there wasn't a speck of red anywhere in the room.

The thing was feeding, hunched over in the middle of the red room with its head bowed over the sloppy, wet carcass of a lamb. Howard walked slowly, almost silently; he had left his shoes at the door of the slaughterhouse, and he could feel the pricks of tiny, fragmented bones dig into his feet through his socks. The slurping sounds of the creature drinking echoed. Howard's eyes flitted up and he saw them, slumped against one wall, the bodies of six women, pale and lifeless. Already, their bellies were fat and bloated. More hooks burst through their throats and their thighs and kept them chained to the wall.

They didn't have to be kept alive, Howard realised. Just *kept*.

He gripped the stake tight and stepped carefully over flaps of brittle skin and the white dust that littered the floor. It felt heavy, wrong in his hands but he had practised, on the scarecrow down at Harry Creed's farm: one firm, quick thrust of the spike through the beast's chest and it was down. It had its back to him – Howard was sure that the stake would work from behind, he would just need to angle it so that it sheared *past* the thing's spine and right into its ribcage.

The sloppy sounds grew louder as he approached and he saw trails of twitching, coiled intestine draped over the creature's slender fingers, saw flecks of meat fall from its mouth in wet, red spittle as it sucked on a pulsing, throbbing ball of wet brown-purple that could only be the lamb's heart. It tore the organ open and thin, white strings inside that looked like the roots of some young, green plant snapped and with long, spiny teeth it dug in, tearing and chewing and drinking.

'Take this, you bitch,' eight-year-old Howard said, thrusting the stake forward with all his might.

The thing had turned before the wooden spike could even reach its back and it grabbed at the shaft of the thing, standing and leering over Howard in one fluid, sickly motion and shoving him back. Howard tumbled, falling into the savaged belly of one of the bovine carcasses on the ground, and bones fell away beneath him.

The creature stood over him and smiled. It had the same wet, sick skin as the one that had taken its sister but its nightmare face was bearded and thin, drawn over a tight, hard skull that pressed outward at its scalp so that Howard could see the lines and indents where the bone curved. It lurched forward so that its face was an inch from his own and its breath smelled like liver.

It glanced down at the cross around Howard's neck and reached down, curling long fingers around the chain. 'If you knew what I really was,' it whispered, 'you would know that *this* doesn't do fuck.'

Howard winced, weight shifting on the meat-deprived carcass beneath him. Its pine curled around his rump, sharp segments digging in through his jeans. His socks were soaked with mucus.

'I haven't drunk from a boy in months,' the thing drawled. It lifted those delicate, pale fingers to Howard's face and brushed his cheek, then its claws gripped his chin and snapped his head upward, exposing his throat. 'You smell good, boy. Calm down. Don't fear me. Fear makes you taste… bitter.'

Howard swallowed.

'Who am I kidding?' the thing hissed, almost laughing. 'You came into my home to kill me.'

175

Its face flashed with anger. Its eyes burned, bloodshot and diseased.

'I don't give a *shit* what you taste like.'

Its mouth cracked open suddenly and Howard watched as a slick tongue danced between rows of long, narrow teeth. It was a mouth that seemed too red and too wide to fit inside that face, like the maw of a snake, and now the tongue was thrashing, flitting from bloody cheek to bloody cheek as the creature lunged forward –

Howard ducked his head to one side, grabbing the creature by the back of its neck and dragging it down so that its flashing teeth buried themselves in the decaying, rotted skin of the cow. The stake plunged upward, into the creature's black-clad belly, and Howard screamed as he drove it upward in one wrenching, rough thrust toward the thing's heart. Splintered wood slid between the thing's ribs and into its chest and it shrieked, spewing torrents of black from its twisted gut onto Howard's throat as it tried to tear itself free.

The beast snapped and snarled and Howard kicked up with a shoeless foot, planting it in the thing's groin. It stumbled back, clutching at the stake in its chest like a wild thing. Blood crashed from the gaping flesh around the wooden spike and it gagged on its own black fluid, hissing and baring its teeth, stained and wet and shining.

Above their heads, one of the Straub sons dangled from his meathook. Blood spattered his bare feet.

A hulking, white shape burst through the fog and plunged its hand into the chest of the nearest creature, tunnelling through the thing's ribs with a sickening *crunch* louder than all the snapping teeth and the thumping of Howard's heart; the abomination wrenched its hand free of the sagging vampire, dragging a fistful of slick, black fluid and throbbing muscle with it. Howard ducked as another of the creatures lunged for him with a red, open mouth and the white-skinned beast from the cellar swiped at its face, carving black lines out of pale flesh with its claws and popping a bloodshot eyeball in a *splotch* of gelatine and sinew. It swung and scratched with long, powerful arms and bellowed, a moaning roar that ruptured from some deep pit in its throat and tore out of the scarred, open mess of its face.

Howard stumbled back, dipping beneath the clawing arm of a black-clothed vampire and tumbling to the floor. The ground was wet and stank of fish and he looked up, toward the back of the room: the great glass wall had been shattered and water was gushing out, flooding over the varnished concrete and swilling through all the blood. The creature from inside the tank had stepped out and it lumbered slowly towards him, shoulders crooked so the left, grey-scaled and peeling so badly that he could see the red skin beneath, dipped beneath the right. Webbed feet slapped the ground and it joined in the guttural cry of the wendigo. In seconds the sharp-toothed creatures had fallen upon it and they scratched and tore at its thighs and its chest like savages, like animals. The aquarium was alive with shrieking hisses and clashing teeth and blue, swimming shadows tossed themselves on the walls and danced madly in the bloody fray.

He crawled toward the door on his elbows and knees, trying not to scream with every agonising movement. The raw skin of his belly dragged on the ground and stretched and he stumbled to his knees, moving like a drunkard, crashing through the bead curtain and out into the store front.

His footsteps were slow and he dragged his aching limbs, sobbing with a closed-up throat as he heard the last, gurgling scream of the thing from the tank, heard the *shhriiikk* of its scaled skin being torn from its body and slurped down by hungry mouths. The white-skinned abomination howled and Howard heard De'Ath screech. A glass pane shattered and wet bodies slapped onto the floor.

There was daylight at the very front of the abandoned little pet shop, slipping in through the glass door and tumbling over dust particles onto the floor. It was beautiful, that golden filtered thrash of light, after the dark, green shadows of the aquarium. Safe. If he could just make it to the door…

Something shrieked and grabbed at his ankle and he

tumbled, grunting as the wind was knocked out of him and his nose cracked on the ground. His vision was thrust into pitch-black for a fraction of a second and in that time the thing crawled onto his back and bit down on the back of his skull, tearing out a great chunk of his scalp. He felt it peel away, felt the hair and the skin torn off the top of his head and turned, forcing an elbow into the thing's chin. He lurched out of its grip, screaming all the while, numb to the pain and the fear and aware only of the fact he had to get out, get to his car. The thing grabbed at him again and he kicked down, stamping his heel onto the thing's wrist and pressing it into the shadows. He tumbled forward and the light fell over his face and then he was out, crashing over the toppled plastic statue-dog and out of the door. His legs knotted over each other and he fell onto the back of the car, crying out as his broken wrist cracked against the metal.

He stood for a second, letting the sunlight wash over his bloody skin and the peeled flesh of his scalp and his torso. Inside he could still hear them screaming, fighting off the rabid beast that he'd brought from downstairs; it was stronger, faster, despite the horrific mutation that had left it deformed, but with so many of them Howard knew it wouldn't last much longer.

Neither would he. He pressed a hand to the back of his skull and it came away slick and sticky. He could smell the meat inside of him pouring out. Even if he called an ambulance he wouldn't make it to the hospital, not now.

He stumbled to the car door and grabbed at the handle. It was locked, but the window was smashed in so he reached in with his arm and broke the catch open. The door fell outward and he slumped in, wincing as every broken bone in him crashed together. Keys still in the ignition. He twisted, hissing as he twisted his good wrist. Lolling in the seat, barely alive or awake, he listened as the sputtering sound of the engine echoed in his ears.

One working hand, two feet that barely wanted to move at all. But he pressed them both down on the gas pedal and the car juddered forward, stuck in first gear and screaming, and as he yanked down the wheel the tyres howled over cracked tarmac.

'I'm sorry, Carrie,' he whispered. 'It was all for you.'

He ground his feet down and plunged the screaming car into the glass front wall of the pet store, jolted upward in his seat as the thing mounted the car and mangled itself in the doorframe. He kept pushing and the Neon's wheels spun rabidly, spitting little flecks of glass and plaster out into the store as the engine roared and it crashed into the aquarium. His foot came off the pedal and the wheels bumped over bone and ground to a halt. Water slapped the tyres.

Through the windscreen, Phobos De'Ath opened his mouth and his teeth flashed in the dark.

Howard smiled back and flicked on the headlamps.

A crackling, brittle wave of purple light thrust out of the front of the car and filled the room. Flares of magenta and sizzling, burnt pink drenched the shadows and all the blood spattered on the walls and swelling in the floodwater on the floor was lit with a white fluorescence.

'UV, you *fuck,*' Howard breathed, and he watched – blood pouring from his head and the stump of his finger and pooled over his stomach, building up in great, damp swathes across his legs – as the creatures began to burn. The screaming turned to one piercing, shrill whine as their eyes bulged and greasy, thin hair smouldered and pale, mucus-coated skin began to bubble and peel in flaking yellow patches.

Everywhere the light touched there was death.

De'Ath's face was a mess of boils and ruptured, shining strips that tore away from his bloodshot eyes and bled down his melting throat.

Dying in the driver's seat, Howard listened to the sound of the moaning engine and the screaming of three dozen leeches as he burned them, and in a flood of blue and purple and shining, electric white, he thought, *this is a peaceful death.*

LEVIATHAN SONG

Below, it waited.

The ocean surface was calm, bright and glittering with the sunlight that danced on swirling, brittle waves. The blue was so intense that any spots of white, gathered in clusters at the crests of rising swells and tumbling into the abysses left in their wake, seemed almost like ice crystals – like they could crack underfoot or break apart with the strike of a pick. Above, the sky was a haze of red and gold as the sun, a fat, bloated orb of white draped in clouds and shimmering at its edges, started to sink beyond the plains and mountains in the distance. Orange drifts flayed the waves and broke the blue into knots of darkened fingers, all grabbing and clutching at the pink-streaked reflection of a dying day.

Below, it *waited.*

Beneath the waves laid an unholy silence, a dark, crushing silence that simmered against the surface and pressed up to the sunlight, that filtered down from sickly, pallid blue to deep royal and further down into the misty grey-green that sifted over the slipping, flitting bodies of silvery fish. Below even that there was darkness; the seabed was miles down, or at least it seemed to be, shrouded by layers of black and grey and oddly-glowing green that streamed in ribbons. Yet, rocks crashed up from the sand, jagged spears of colour that broached this shroud of dark and pierced the blue, strung with algae and decayed corals and the littered wreckage of a million dead things. The rocks were a crown of spines in the depths and even they seemed to peel back from it, like if it grew any wider or any more fiercely quiet they would crumble away and gladly fall into the black.

It hung sixty feet below the surface of the water, untouched by the sunlight but cradled in its own searing glow; tendrils of light seemed to brush their fingers over its single, curled edge and recoil, falling over the points of the rocks below and scrambling beyond them in some mad dash to hide from it. It pulsed, like a heartbeat, the heartbeat of some long-dead thing – slow, calm, and emanating a strange heat with every thrumming vibration.

Fish investigated the thing, skittering close to it only to dart away as the face of it looked upon them. It was featureless and hollow, but there was a sense of unease that came with staring at it, as if it was staring right back.

For days it lay undiscovered by human eyes, and then a small fishing boat carrying three men and a thirty-kilogramme haul of seabass and whiting disappeared as it passed over the thing, sucked beneath by some horrific, unseen force in a swirling screw of saltwater and sunlight. The decayed skeleton of one of the men was discovered six weeks after, washed ashore eighty miles south; the flesh had rotted at an incredible and unprecedented rate, leaving the bones completely clean, and even they had begun to erode to a level that made it almost impossible to determine the barnacle-encrusted carcass's identity. There was a small colony of fish rooted in his skull, the species of which could not be determined, although they appeared to be some cross between a starfish and a small tuna, with their bodies slim and blue and their tails a spiralling mess of points. They had no eyes or mouths, and they had all been born (it seemed) and died inside his head.

In that time, a kilometre-wide stretch of ocean around the thing was cordoned off and half a dozen small military vessels assigned to watch over the perimeter in shifts. A plan to research and analyse it was devised, although volunteers for the project were difficult to find.

Below, it waited.

And below *it,* deep in the shadows beyond the salt-corroded rock piles and the green mist, something moved. Something huge and slow, a behemoth of some forbidden, undersea world that was just as patient.

'Alright, going down,' Karlsson said, clamping a bulky set of headphones over his ears.

Morrison nodded, lifting her gloved hand to the ceiling and flicking switches along a red-lit bank inches above her head. 'Twenty feet,' she replied, cranking a lever on the panel before her seat. 'Thirty.'

'Hey, Kel, pressure okay?'

Across the little room, pressed in by metal walls scattered with screens and rows of bulbs, Kelly Allen nodded. 'All good.' She was the Pretty One, Morrison thought, all blonde, straight lifts of hair pinned to her scalp and tight features on a stern, narrow face. Even in the standard-issue boiler suit she looked good. Christ knew how Karlsson or the other guys would cope if they knew about all her degrees.

'Forty,' Morrison said, eyes firmly fixed on the depth gauge in front of her. She could see her reflection in the glass but ignored it, gaze drifting to the right so as not to make eye contact with the face on the screen. A little crack slipped between her nose and her lips so that her chin was jolted a bit to the side. Dim, green eyes glittered in the grey light. 'Fifty-five. Sixty.'

'Nothing on the radar yet,' another voice chimed in. A low, salt-sifted voice. 'Has the bastard thing moved again?'

'Not gonna show on the radar, is it, Colin?' Kelly said. 'You'll have to use the cameras.'

'Fucking thing's basically a black hole,' Karlsson said. 'Use your head, Col.'

Morrison smiled a little. Behind her, Colin grunted. 'Dutch prick telling me to use my head,' he murmured. 'Nothing on camera either. Little deeper.'

'Eighty feet,' Morrison said.

'I'm Swedish,' Karlsson said, running a hand through thick, yellow hair as he stood up and crossed to the middle of the room. 'Colin, keep an eye on that camera. Morrison – sorry, what was your first name?'

'Nancy,' Morrison said quietly. 'Ninety feet.'

'Nancy. Halt descent when we get close. Kel, you got everything else covered?'

'Tell me you're not already busting for a piss,' Colin said.

'Fuck off,' Karlsson said, moving to the door. The sub remained steady. The ground beneath Morrison's boots hummed. 'Looks like we're getting some weird temperature readings, I'm gonna check the sensors.'

'What else were we expecting?' Colin said. 'Thing's throwing off all sorts of heat.'

'Be careful,' Morrison said as Karlsson cranked a wheel on the door and stepped through.

'Scared, Nance?' Kelly grinned.

Morrison turned her head and smiled back. 'You're not?'

The door shut with a *clang* and she turned back to her display, listening as Karlsson's footsteps grew quieter down the hall. The sub was small, but long – initially, they had planned to go down in a little two-man research vessel, but after the thing (they were calling it the Hole, back on the surface) started to shift depths every couple of hours, disappearing and reappearing a few metres deeper and a few farther South every time, they found themselves in need of something capable of withstanding a little more pressure. The S-Class *Marginis* felt safer too, a long, torpedo-shaped shell of sleek, grey metal.

'He's gone to piss, I'll put a tenner on it,' Colin said.

'Poor excuse,' Kelly agreed.

'Passing a hundred feet. No sign yet, Col?'

'No sign. And we're not on first names yet, Morrison. Make it through this and a couple more trips and we'll see.'

'Don't know your last,' Morrison said. Red hair fell in her face. She brushed it out of her eyes. 'Hundred-and-ten.'

'Just call him shithead till he learns a little respect,' Kelly said. 'Just as rude to me, first time we went below.'

'You're rude,' Colin snapped.

The door opened and Karlsson stepped back in, fumbling with the zip on his boiler suit.

'Ha! Told you,' Colin said. 'Bastard went for a little wee-wee, didn't he?'

'Shut it, shithead,' Karlsson said, moving to his seat and slumping down into it.

'See?' Kelly said. 'Perfect name for him.

'Hundred-thirty.'

The depth gauge flickered.

'Visual on camera.'

'Show me,' Karlsson said, spinning round in his seat and leaning forward to glance at Colin's screen. 'Alright, Nancy, halt us there. Kel, start running diagnostic.'

'Running.'

'Can I see?' Morrison said, turning her head.

'We hanging?'

'Hanging.'

'Then sure, come take a look. Quickly.'

Morrison scurried up from her seat and crossed the tight space, almost crouching in front of Colin's control panel. He was bearded and scruffy and smelled like cigarette smoke. She grimaced and watched the screen, eyes widening.

'It's beautiful,' she said.

'It's a fucking circle,' Colin said.

'No, she's right.' Karlsson shook his head, looking up at her. They caught eyes for a moment and she smiled. 'It *is* beautiful.'

It shimmered on the screen, a flat, black disc hovering in the blue. Golden mist seemed to seep from its edges and dissipate into the saltwater and it was held in a ring of dazzling, writhing lights, but its mouth was the purest, darkest black she had ever seen.

'Can we get any closer to it?' Morrison said.

'Kel, we getting good readings from there?'

'We're getting *readings*. Don't know about good, but they're solid enough.'

'Then I think we're close enough,' Karlsson said, smiling up apologetically. 'Don't want to risk anything until we know it's safe.'

'Again,' Colin said, '*circle.* What's it gonna do, Dutch-boy?'

The submarine juddered. Morrison jolted up and her skull smacked the ceiling. 'Ow!' she said. The vessel had stopped shaking but the floor shivered. Something slid off a desk in the hall and shattered on the floor.

'Bollocks,' Karlsson said, turning to his controls. 'The fuck was that?'

Morrison's hand went to her hair and came away warm and sticky. Blood slid down the back of her neck.

'Shit, Nance, you alright?' Kelly said, looking up from her readings.

'Dutch-boy,' Colin said quietly. 'Does that thing look a little bigger to you?'

Morrison looked at the screen. The circle had grown, a gaping, shining maw extending into the blue.

'Have we moved, Nancy?' Karlsson said.

She turned back to her own display, shook her head. 'If we have, we're only a couple of metres closer to it.'

When she turned around again, Karlsson was standing over her, glancing over the mess of her scalp. 'That hurt?' he said softly. 'We've got a first-aid kit in here somewhere, if you need something –'

'I'm fine,' she smiled, laying a hand on his arm. 'Thank you.'

He smiled back.

'Hey, lovebirds,' Kelly said. 'Think we've got enough? Don't know about you lot, but this thing creeps me out. I'm ready to head back up top.'

Karlsson leant forward, plucking a pair of reading glasses out of his breast pocket and slipping them on. 'Wow.'

'Yeah,' Kelly said.

'What is it?'

'Thing's toxic, Nance,' Kelly shook her head. 'Not just *heat* it's spitting out, there's some kind of radioactive element to it – I'm not sure we're even safe this close to it, even in this thing – that, and the spatial density of this thing, it won't show up on the radar, like it doesn't even exist, but it's *heavy* –'

'Fuck!' Colin yelled as another wave of movement rocked the sub. The whole thing seemed to tilt backwards as it groaned and the walls shuddered. He tumbled forward in his chair and his palm struck the control panel.

When the vessel stopped moving, Morrison realised she was holding Karlsson's arm again. He squeezed her hand. 'Yeah, let's bring her back up,' he said. 'Colin, tell me the Hole didn't pull us closer again.'

Silence. Outside, something moved in the deep.

'Colin?'

'Look at this,' Colin said.

Karlsson looked. 'The hell is that?'

'That can't be right,' Morrison said. 'That's… what is that, right below us?'

Colin nodded. 'I bumped the controls. Switched cameras. This is the one plastered to the belly of the sub. So we're looking… straight down.'

'It's the same model,' Kelly said. 'The exact same.'

'Not quite,' Karlsson said. 'Look at the rust on that thing, it's fifty years old. Sixty, at a push.'

Morrison stepped closer. On the screen, jagged, brittle rock formations broke free of the grip of deep, black shadow, cradled in mist. The image was blurred and it crackled a little, and there was a spot of moisture on the inside of the camera so that a cluster of pixels in the top right corner was melted and warped, but she could see it clearly, broken on the rocks; a submarine, split clean in half so that its wreckage was separated and branched upward like two barnacle-driven husks. Claws of scrap metal thrashed up from the mangled wreck and silverfish darted between them.

'Go back to the other screen,' Morrison said quietly.

Colin didn't move.

'Col, do what she says,' Karlsson said. 'We have to see.'

Slowly, Colin jabbed a button on the bank of controls and the screen flickered and changed.

'Shit,' Kelly breathed. 'We have to get above water. Now.'

'Agreed,' Colin said.

The Hole had spread again, widened so that it almost filled the screen. It flitted and twisted, golden rings moving and shifting around it like it was waking up. Even the pitch-black centre of the thing seemed to have deepened, like it was panning out – like it was a throat opening wider and wider to take them in.

'Up,' Karlsson said. 'Get us up, now.'

Morrison couldn't move. There was something hypnotic about the way it moved, something beautiful in the shining tendrils that crashed about its bleeding, black gums, that captured her and forced her to watch.

'Nance, bring us back up,' Kelly said.

Morrison blinked. 'Right,' she said, turning to her controls. 'Starting ascent –'

Something crashed against the outside of the sub and the whole thing tipped to one side. Kelly cried out as she was thrust into the control bank and there was a horrific, wrenching groan as some part of the vessel tore in on itself. Morrison grabbed for Karlsson's arm but he had fallen and she tumbled too, busting her ankle on the back of her chair and sliding into the wall.

On the screen, the Hole reached out to them with long, black arms and pulled them closer. The submarine shook and trembled and rolled forward. Colin was yanked from his chair and he cracked his head on the ceiling. Kelly screamed.

He fell, limp, on top of Morrison and his head snapped round so that he was looking right at her with wide, blood-splashed eyes. Inches from her face, his mouth fell open and he lolled forward.

'He's dead!' she yelled. 'Oh my god, he's fucking –
'

The walls of the sub creaked and moaned and howled as some unseen force tried to compress it. Suddenly they were hurtling forward, dragged by the black tendrils of the void in the saltwater as golden lights crashed and danced on the screen. The vessel tipped over again, rolling on its back, and Karlsson fell to the ceiling. There was a horrible splintering and he screamed as his spine thrust forward and down into his hips.

'Kel, strap in to something!' Morrison yelled.

'Jesus Christ!' Kelly yelled. 'Karlsson, are you –'

'Kelly! Hold on, for fuck's sake!'

The engines juddered and a fierce heat seared the bridge and suddenly Morrison was on her back, somewhere in the little room, legs splayed over hot metal and screaming as it pressed against her palms and seared the flesh. The screen was black and sizzling and the Hole seemed to be spitting fire onto the skin of the sub as it dragged it forward and *down* –

Everything stopped moving.

Morrison panted, looking up. The black had disappeared from the screen and all she could see was thick, murky water. Greener than before. Much greener, like all the topaz blue had been stripped from it and filled in with some sickly, cambium floodlight.

Shadows moved around them in the water.

'Karlsson?' Kelly said, crawling across the floor towards him.

He groaned. Morrison looked; blood pooled over the hip of his boiler suit and something hard poked up against the material where she imagined the bone had broken through his skin.

'Don't try to move him,' she said.

'Is Colin okay?' Karlsson grunted. He hissed through his teeth as pain shot up his spine.

'No,' Morrison said. 'Stay there. We'll get help. We'll…'

'Nance?'

Morrison swallowed.

'Nance, what is it?'

'There's something down there,' she breathed, nodding toward the screen.

The camera was pointed down, into the dark, and molten shadows writhed and crackled in the mire.

'Of course there's something down there,' Kelly murmured, cradling her head. 'It's the sea, there's probably *millions* of –'

'No, something big.'

Karlsson moaned. 'Can you get us back up? We need to…'

He balked, face whitening, and vomited onto his boiler suit. Blood-streaked teeth flashed in the glaring red lights. Morrison realised a siren was blaring somewhere in the sub, muffled by the steady drip of blood in the bridge and the crushing dark outside.

She turned back to her controls and frowned. 'We're deeper,' she said. Her chest was pounding. 'It didn't just pull us forward, it… pulled us down.'

'Did you feel us go down?' Kelly said.

'Does it matter?' Karlsson spat. 'Get us to the surface before we all end up like Colin!'

'Have some respect,' Kelly said quietly. Her eyes were fixed on Colin's shattered skull. His eyes were wide and angry and looking right at her.

'It doesn't make any sense,' Morrison said, shaking her head. Her fingers hovered over the controls. 'We're way below a hundred-forty feet down, but the coordinates are exactly the same.'

Kelly hobbled to Colin's screen and jabbed a button so that the display changed. 'Rock formations look the same,' she said. 'We haven't moved.'

'So what, the sea level's gone up?' Morrison said. 'What about the water, are your readings any different?'

'What the *fuck* does it matter?' Karlsson yelled. He tried to sit up and his back *crack*ed. He screamed.

'Don't move, for god's sake!' Kelly said.

'Get us to the fucking surface *now,* or I could die in this room and the two of you will be left to deal with this on your own.'

'And we're not capable?' Morrison cocked an eyebrow.

'My *back* is broken, give me a shitting break! Bring us up and get us to a fucking hospital –'

'I don't think that's possible,' Morrison said quietly.

Kelly blinked. 'What?'

Morrison looked back at them and smiled sadly. 'I don't think there *is* an up anymore. Think about it: the water level's risen – it must have, because we haven't moved an *inch* – the water out there's completely different, I can see the readings from here, not to mention the *colour,* and that thing down there…'

Kelly glanced at the screen. It moved in the dark, drifting slowly at the roots of the rocks and throwing shadows over the blistering algae.

'That's not like any fish I've ever seen.'

'What the piss are you saying?' Karlsson grunted.

'You're not serious,' Kelly said. 'You can't be suggesting –'

Morrison nodded. 'That hole was a doorway. We've gone through.'

'Through to where?' Karlsson said. 'Am I the only one who doesn't have a fucking *clue* what you're saying?'

'Not where,' Morrison said. 'When.'

On the screen, a tentacle lashed up from the dark.

'Fuck off,' Karlsson said.

'She's right,' Kelly said, scrolling through the cameras. 'Readings are way off. Water out there's almost toxic. To us, anyway. And colder than before.'

'Where's it gone?' Morrison said. 'The Hole.'

'That's what I'm looking for,' Kelly said. 'Nothing yet…'

The view on the screen flickered, changing from a glittering crest of rock piles to a hazy, blank pall of dirty green. Nothing moved; even the swill of the sunlight seemed softer. Everything was silent.

'It's gone,' Kelly whispered.

'There's no way back?'

'Come on,' Karlsson grunted, clutching at his bloody hip. His hand trembled. 'There's no such thing as time travel. And it doesn't happen like *this*.'

Kelly jabbed the button again.

The tentacle thrust up toward the camera and a flash of purple filled the screen, split in half by a jagged crack across the lens. The sub shook as something smacked its belly and Karlsson hissed in pain. '*Jesus!*'

The screen went black.

'Fuck!' Kelly yelled. 'Get us up, Nance!'

Morrison scrambled with the controls, yanking back the lever that would bring them rising to the surface. The sub strained against something and she shook her head, blood thumping in her ears. 'It's got hold of us!'

'Can we call for help?' Kelly said.

'Not below the surface,' Morrison said. 'We'd have to get above water and raise the antenna –'

'Try it!' Karlsson grunted.

Something heavy thumped the wall behind Morrison's head and she yelped as a long, wide dent spread across the metal.

'What the fuck is it, then?' Karlsson yelled. 'Is that thing a fucking dinosaur?'

'I don't know!' Morrison cried, shooting him a look. She rammed down the lever and the vessel strained against a thick, crushing weight but didn't move. Behind her, the radio hissed.

'Come in!' Kelly said. 'Come in, this is the *Marginis* reporting external damage, one crewmember down, requesting assistance! Mayday, mayday!'

Nothing but a hiss of static.

'Try another channel!' Karlsson yelled. Outside, something crashed against the pointed nose of the sub and metal wrenched and groaned.

'There's nobody out there!' Morrison said. 'If that thing's some prehistoric… I don't fucking know – who the fuck can we call for help?'

'Mayday!' Kelly yelled. Something creaked. Down below, way down in the water, a low, long moan sounded. Like the song of a whale, except this was deeper, somehow sorrowful and beautiful and haunting. 'Mayday, there's something here –'

With a crackling, electronic *pshhh,* a voice crept through the speakers.

'...*непризнанный корабль*...'

'What the – is that *Russian?*'

'...*ближе и будем стрелять торпедами*...'

'Turn it off!' Morrison yelled.

Karlsson nodded at the screen. 'I know my subs,' he said quietly. 'That's been out of service for years.'

Morrison looked. On the screen, a deep, grey smudge grew closer, drawing towards them and looming in the dark.

'...*Господи, что, черт возьми, это?*'

'That's Cold War era,' Karlsson breathed. 'That's a fucking Cold War vessel.'

'So if that thing isn't a dinosaur,' Morrison said, 'what the *fuck* is it, and how long has it been down –'

Suddenly the sub wrenched apart. Metal screamed and the door shattered inwards and within seconds the whole room had flooded with water. Morrison opened her mouth to scream as Kelly's body shot out the door, crashing against the frame on its way out and flopping into the green murk. A flash of purple seared past the opening in a blur and she gripped onto her chair but already the current and the thrusting swell of the water was dragging her out and then

for a moment
she was floating.

Everything seemed to happen so slowly.

Kelly's body disappeared, swallowed by the sea in the shadow of the advancing Soviet submarine. Morrison could still hear the Russians on the radio, yelling and screaming as they watched the carnage unfold, as they watched the *Marginis* fall apart, split in two and torn open like a dead, leaden Christmas cracker. The nose half of the vessel had already started to fall and it sank to the rocks, crashing in a cloud of silt-grey smoke and toppling onto its end, clawed, broken-metal fingers reaching up to grasp at the monster that had shredded its guts open.

Blood drifted from Karlsson's boiler suit as water filled it and she watched him screaming and thrashing as the creature reached for him.

It was beautiful.

Morrison struggled as saltwater pushed into her mouth and down her throat, filling up her lungs. She wanted to choke and to vomit and to spit it all out but she could do nothing except grab at her neck and kick out her legs in a furious attempt to reach the surface. The pressure was incredible and she felt it pressing in against her skull and her ribs, knew that her spine had already been severed and crushed inward, and she thought that she might have broken her legs on the way out of the sub but it didn't matter, none of it mattered. Not the cold that sheared her flesh and seeped into her blood or the muted sounds all around, the screeching and the howling and the roaring and the moaning and the gurgling scream that she *knew,* somehow was her –

None of it.

The creature was endless, a writhing mass of purple and blue and colours she had never seen before. Its skin shimmered, shining and shifting and curling around the coiled limbs of thick, tree-trunk tentacles that whipped and thrashed in all the broken mess of the sea. It was sprawled among the rocks and the water, stuffing Karlsson with one sucker-strewn arm into a ringed maw full of barbed teeth and bright, red gums, rows and rows of them all spiralling down into a throat as deep and as black as the Hole that had dragged them to its nest. In less than a second – a second that would, Morrison thought, have lasted for an eternity if it had not been interrupted – the creature had turned a tentacle on her and she realised that the pressure around her waist was not from the depth but from the grip of a thick, coiled barrel of an arm. It dragged her into its mouth and in that last fraction of a sun-smeared second she saw its eye, a great, shining disc of pure black ringed with gold and purple and dotted with starlight.

It sang as it closed its teeth around her and – just for a moment, before the rigid, bloody gums around her neck clamped down and separated her head from her body, held there in dark by the barbs and with the smell of salt and fish and death in her nose – she could *breathe.*

X238
(THE RAGE: PART TWO)

The briefcase lay flat on his bedside cabinet, clasp shining in the moonlight that sifted in through the window. It had laid there since his last day of work, untouched but tempting. His bed was empty, the sheets pressed and tucked into the corners of a sweat-slicked mattress. The light was on, and it flickered every time he moved about in the attic, frayed cord swinging as the floorboards above the ceiling groaned. It glinted off the corners of the case and shivered on the edges of a black, metal cross hung on the wall. The cross was pinned right above the headboard of the bed and a deep, grey shadow peeled from it down the plaster.

The house was quiet, except for the low murmur in the attic; the only sounds were the steady drip of a tap in the kitchen and the squeal of the ladder on the landing, hanging from rusted hinges set into the attic trapdoor and swaying gently back and forth like a pendulum.

'What am I supposed to do, then?' Freddie moaned,

on his knees amongst all the cobwebs and dust mites, dark-skinned face draped in the shadows from the crossbeams over his head. There was a window in the attic but it had been boarded over, a black, plastic sheet pinned to the glass and pressed against it with wooden slats. He looked up, eyes wild and round with fear. 'Tell me. Please, what do I do?'

There was no answer. Jesus Christ watched him, bloody, from the crucifix leant against the wall, eight feet tall and carved out of splintered, varnished wood. Thick strands of webbing danced around the crown of thorns on his head and dripped from his beard in long, flowing strings. His eyes were blank. He was the work of a gay couple out in the country; Freddie had commissioned it specially. Crosses were scattered around the attic, nailed to the beams and dangling from chains in the slanted ceiling so that they hung and spun around his head. Long shadows drifted over Freddie's bare shoulders and slid down his back.

'Please,' Freddie said, lurching forward and laying his palms flat on the floorboards. He dug his nails into the wood and pressed his forehead down, sobbing into the mess of a white, long cross he'd painted along the floor. Naked and crying and curled into a ball, Freddie rocked back and forth and said, 'Why? Why did you take her?'

First, it was the job. He had worked with that company right since his last day of medical school, stuck with them all through their year-long bout of near-bankruptcy despite all the offers from other companies. And when they started to work with the cruder, more ambiguous drugs he stuck with them because finally they were out of debt and they gave him a raise. He ploughed through as they tested X237 on rats and kittens and worms, watched the animals go insane with every injection and anal administration and did so with a callous unfeeling because now they were paying him five figures a year. When they started dragging people off the street he said nothing.

When it all went wrong, he lost the job. The company went under. X237 was destroyed. All of it.

And then he lost Wendy.

He had never told her, about all of the things they'd paid him to do, because she'd hate him. Little Wendy had always looked up to her big brother and he couldn't let her down, not like that. She'd call him a monster.

But then she disappeared, and Freddie was left jobless and alone and drained with grief and anger and guilt and sorrow and *rage* and some unbridled, unhinged passion to kill himself and he knew he could *do* it, knew the cancer would get him anyway in five or six years so why wait?

But he had something.

In his bedroom, the briefcase glinted in the swinging, crackling light.

'I can't,' Freddie said, turning onto his back and

spreading his arms, lying, as Christ had lain, on the cross with his hands pinned to the bars and his ankles twisted together in some damp, sweaty knot; his skin was drenched with beads of salt and his chest rose and fell with every breath and he looked up, at the ring of crosses hung above him, watched them dance in the dark. 'I couldn't.'

It was stronger than the last batch. It was raw, strung together from a mess of ingredients pure and whole enough to destroy each other in the mix if Freddie hadn't figured it all out. X238 was the one. X237 had failed, had turned animals insane and rabid and made men into monsters. Freddie had worked it out and when the company finally went down, he brought it home.

The briefcase was locked, but the key for the padlock lay right beside it on the bedside table.

Freddie showered, washing off the dust and the webbing and letting it swirl around his feet into the plughole. Hot water rose around him and he laid his hands on the tiles, slick palms spread flat and waiting as he bowed his head, eyes closed, and let the heat crash over his shoulders. At his feet the little metal-ringed whirlpool had stopped spinning, clogged with a mess of brown and grey and all the white paint that had stuck to his skin and peeled from him now in strips. The water rose around his soles and he turned his head, saw it, at the other end of the bathroom, obscured by the haze of dripping water and steam in his eyes: a cracked, dented oil drum, top spewing flames into the alleyway, and wasted hands hovered above it, fingerless gloves fraying and burning in the heat.

The van reeled into the alley and stopped, back doors swinging open. It was black, inside. One of the men in the street looked up from the fire but the others were too focused on it to even notice the thing. His eyes widened. He cried out.

They burst out of the cab, two of them, dressed in black with masks covering their faces so that only the hungry, white slits of their eyes showed through. Freddie was in the back of the van; he had asked to come along – he was in Development, it wasn't his job to round up the test subjects, but he had wondered whether their sourcing might have something to do with the fact all the tests ended so fucking *horribly* – and now that he saw where the subjects were coming from, he found himself strangely undisturbed by the fact. He watched as the men in black bundled the screaming innocents into the van, stinking of smoke and grease, and he realised he had known all along, to some degree.

Freddie collapsed under the weight of the water and doubled over, grasping at the edge of the bathtub with one hand as his throat tore up and a mess of deep, wet coughing erupted from his lips. Blood splashed the ceramic and mixed in with the water. The plughole was blocked and the blood rose above his feet, splashing his ankle as he rolled back and his head hit the tiles. He yelled something and blood flew from his tongue as the sputtering thrashed about in his lungs. His teeth were stained with it and splashed with it and he grinned, lips peeling upward. He fumbled for the shower head and pointed it away from himself and listened, as the water started to spatter the tiled floor of the bathroom and soak into all the towels. The cancer shredding his lungs was cruel and it stung his oesophagus but he smiled through it and the smile turned to laughter, a bitter, blood-soaked laughter that echoed.

Crashing, half-blind with all the shampoo and hot water in his eyes, Freddie reared up from the blood and lurched towards the sink with a trembling arm, grabbing at the razor nestled against his toothbrush. He recoiled and popped the blade from the thing, clutching it between his palms and lifting them in prayer.

'Our father,' he started, and his throat ruptured in another fit of coughing. 'Our father, who art in the attic and under the ground, listening to me fucking *die* up here – fuck you!' he yelled, laughing all the while, every word punctuated by the deep, horrible cackle of a madman and the sputtering of someone with very little to lose.

Suddenly the blade was pressed between his thumb and index finger and he dragged it down his chest by the point, drawing a long, vertical line in the dark skin so that beads of blood swam up to the surface and dribbled down to his groin. The cut slid all the way down his sternum and down through his abdomen and when he had reached his pelvis he plucked the blade from his skin and dipped it in the putrid shower water at his feet.

'Fuck you!' he yelled, lifting the blade again and piercing the skin at the left side of his belly. With one swift, stinging arc he had drawn a second line across his gut, left to right, and he dropped the blade by his feet and let the blood wash over him, spewing from a red, upside-down cross on his torso.

The cuts weren't deep enough to damage him but the feeling was incredible and the laughter grew louder and stronger as the coughing faded. The agony in his lungs was replaced by a new, brighter kind of pain, one that stung and burned and pushed up into his throat with some fiery abandon. His hand, smeared with red, slipped between his legs and he caressed his own hardness, laughter turning from a harsh cackle to the childish, high-pitched giggle of a schoolchild.

When Freddie had finished he dragged mothballs out of the plughole with his fingers and let the water and the blood and his wretched seed swirl down into the drain. He dried himself off and crossed the hall to his bedroom, naked save for the towel wrapped around his waist. It was stained red from the mess on his chest and the cuts cracked and stung with every step. Flicking on the light in his room, he stepped over to the bed and sat on the edge of the mattress. He fumbled with a pack of cigarettes on the bedside table and drew one, laying back and letting the smoke rise above him and cloud his eyes.

Suddenly he shot forward, reaching for the briefcase with the cigarette still dangling out of his lips. He lifted it onto his lap and brushed the lid with his hands, leaving a faint track of red on the metal. Slowly, he slid the key into the padlock and cast it aside, opening the case so the faint light above his head drifted across the contents.

They were packed in sponge and nestled amongst each other so their tips all pointed inward: six identical syringes, six carefully-measured doses. The fluid glittered inside six glass tubes like petrol, viscous and translucent and almost tinted with gold. The needles shone.

Freddie's eyes turned up to the ceiling. 'I've nothing else,' he said quietly.

The cancer would destroy him before long – much sooner than all the doctors had estimated, he knew that. The money would run out and they'd shut off his electricity and his water and leave him in debt with nothing but darkness and cold for comfort, and *Wendy* was gone, delightful, wonderful little-brat-sister Wendy, and –

Before he knew what he'd done, the syringe was in

his hand. He raised it to the light, eyeing the glistening serum within. For years they'd been striving for something perfect, something that could increase a man's strength, better define his thoughts, make him *better*. For years. And X238 was all his, now the company had gone under. All that remained of it were these six syringes and a deliciously-complex recipe in his head nobody would ever be able to replicate – nobody but Freddie.

This shit would make him rich.

But it had never been tested. The project was shut down before they could roll it into phase one and none of the partners were brave enough to take it on afterwards; they just destroyed everything and ran.

Cowards.

Freddie smiled. He squeezed out a little of the serum and watched it bead on the hair-fine point of the needle. Slowly, delicately, he lifted the needle to the back of his neck and closed his eyes as the cool metal pressed against his flesh.

Stronger. Faster. Fitter.

His thumb lingered on the plunger. His teeth flashed in the pale light of the room, blood peeling from the inverted cross on his chest.

What if it kills me?

He paused, drawing the needle back a little. His eyes snapped open. There were six syringes; he could afford a couple of trials before his own. Some part of him was desperate for the serum; perhaps, along with everything else, it would cure him. The side effects of X237 had included some internal cellular aggression – healthy cells turned on the weak and the mutated and consumed them, destroyed them, duplicating themselves in some unnatural process of rapid regeneration and evolution that burned out all the sick and frail and replaced them with strong, new cells. Maybe his lungs would reject the cancer and cast it aside in clumps of shrivelled nothing.

The other part of him was afraid. He had seen the last test results. On paper, and in the flesh. And he was rational, he told himself. He could respect the process.

Slowly, Freddie slid the syringe back into the briefcase and closed the lid.

Freddie found his test subject in the alleyway behind the April Leaf Library, clawing the guts out of a rotted rat carcass and shovelling them into his mouth.

'Hey,' Freddie called. He stood at the mouth of the alley and clutched the briefcase with knotted fingers. He had dressed in a suit and tie and the buttons scratched against the raw skin of his torso. He blinked as the homeless man looked up, all wiry grey hair and sagging flesh taped to brittle, bruised bones. The old man was wearing a ragged, green Puffa jacket and baggy jeans and the beanie hat that had tousled his hair was clutched in one bloody hand.

'Whattayouwant?' the man grunted.

Freddie stepped forward and his shadows loomed on the wall of the alley. The old man's eyes darted from side to side. Freddie raised a hand and smiled. 'Don't worry,' he said. 'I'm not going to hurt you. I want to show you something.'

The man gave him a sceptical look, but said nothing.

'Is that okay?' Freddie said. He stopped beside the old man and laid the briefcase down on top of a battered, wooden crate at the edge of the alleyway. The wood was damp and scarred and a steady drip of filthy rain streamed from a sagging gutter above.

'Change?' said the old man.

Freddie smiled, slipping a hand into his jacket and pulling out a crisp twenty-pound note. 'How about this?' he said, offering the thing. Cold wind bit at his hand; it drifted down the alley, dragging up a stink from the rat carcass on the floor and the glittering shards of scattered needles.

Ratty fingers snatched the note and gripped it tight.

'Perfect,' Freddie said, smiling a little. He turned, wiping the hand on his trousers, and unclasped the briefcase. The syringes inside glinted in the light.

The old man was behind him suddenly, looking into the case. 'Oh, no, I ain't got money for none a that, sir, I c'n hardly afford a sanwich or nothin – you oughtta take these somewhere else, get lotsa money for em.'

'Oh, this is free,' Freddie said. He picked up the syringe he had almost planted in his own neck and offered it for the man to see. It hung in the creases of his palm and rolled a little. 'This is medicine. The kind of medicine that could cure anything.'

He swallowed. The lie felt sticky on his tongue but it felt good, too, to say it.

'What do you think? Do you want to give it a try?'

'I ain't got shitall wrong wi me,' the man said, taking a stumbling step back. His ankle cracked the rat carcass' spine and bloody flesh popped under the weight of his foot. 'Sorry, mister, I don't need nothin like –'

Freddie grabbed the man by his lapel and yanked him close, blood thumping in his ears as impatience and frustration pulsed in his chest. 'Shut the fuck up and take it,' he hissed, thrusting the fingers of his free hand into the man's greasy hair and popping his head back to expose a narrow, veiny throat. He jammed the syringe into the homeless man's flesh and stepped back as he gagged and spat. The needle had drawn blood but the aim was perfect; right in the vein. The syringe wiggled, jutting out of the man's neck as he stumbled back and dropped to his knees.

The twenty-pound note fluttered out of his hand as his arms twitched and convulsed violently and he gasped for air, eyes widening. His veins throbbed and popped out of his neck and his temples. 'What have you… wha –'

The man fell to his face and the syringe rattled on the concrete. For a moment the body jerked about uncontrollably, arms and legs kicking out, and then it was still.

Completely, inevitably still.

Freddie ran a hand over his bald, dark-skinned head and let out a breath of disappointment. Slowly, he stepped forward and crouched beside the body, pressing two fingers to a blood-smeared throat. He waited, listened.

Nothing.

'Shit,' he said, monotone, and he stood and turned back to the briefcase.

The lid clasped shut and Freddie started to walk away, carrying it by his waist and kicking away the fallen syringe. He bent down to pick up the twenty-pound note and folded it into his pocket. He half-considered tossing the briefcase into a waste bin on his way home. X238 was useless to him, now.

The old man coughed.

Freddie froze. After a moment he turned his head, looking back over his shoulder. The old man was sitting up, hand pressed to his temple. He groaned, like he had a headache, and coughed again. Flecks of blood hit the tarmac.

Freddie set the briefcase down and walked back, slowly, bent down a little so he could see better in the shadows. 'Hey,' he said, 'are you alright?'

The man looked all around himself, fingering the little red hole in his neck gently. 'Where am... who are you? The fuck did you do to me?'

Freddie smiled. The man was lurching to his feet and he looked fine. Colour blushed his cheeks beneath wiry stubble and his eyes had lost some of their milky sheen. 'How are you feeling?' Freddie said.

'You gave me the medicine,' the man said slowly. He looked down at his hands, like he was half-expecting them to glow or shimmer. 'I feel...'

'Yes?' Freddie said, taking a step closer.

The man smiled up at him. 'I feel *good,*' he said. 'I feel... clean.'

'Oh, amazing,' Freddie grinned. Relief flooded him. 'Oh, brilliant.'

It worked.

The man was shrugging off his green coat, rubbing his arms a little. 'I don't feel cold no more,' he said. Beneath the coat a frayed black t-shirt covered a scrawny chest and his narrow, bony arms were bare. There was a silver cross around his throat that looked stained with dirt and blood and eroded at the edges by water. 'I feel *warm.* On the inside. I feel strong. The fuck is that stuff, doc?'

Freddie laughed. 'Oh, this is fucking brilliant!' he yelled. 'You're going to make me fucking –'

Crack

Freddie looked down and his eyes widened. The old man's fingers jerked suddenly and with another *crack* lengthened, splintering and splitting open. Two fingernails on his right hand splintered. The man frowned.

'What's… ah, shit, that hurts,' he said.

Freddie shook his head. 'No, no, no, what hurts? Nothing's supposed to hurt, what *hurts?*'

The man opened his mouth to speak. His jaw cracked and shot forward, bones in his skull thrusting out and pushing against his skin. His eyes bulged as the brows twisted and forced his lids down. Thin lips peeled back and his teeth jutted up out of bleeding gums, sliding right out to the roots and grinding together so harshly Freddie thought they might all be pushed out into his mouth. The old man gagged on blood and clutched at his throat with long, clawed fingers.

Freddie stepped back. 'No, no, no…'

Suddenly the man's bones wrenched themselves outward: white shafts of skeleton crashed out of his elbows, severing the flesh and bursting out of him in a spray of blood; he doubled over and his shoulderblades pressed against the fabric of the shirt as his legs shivered and his knees smacked the ground.

'Oh god,' Freddie said, '*no…*'

He wanted to run but he was frozen to the spot, helpless but to watch as the old man transformed, skin peeling off like the brittle shedding of a snake and fluttering away on the wind, revealing wet, red muscle beneath. His spine thrashed and writhed and *crack*ed upwards and the bones jutted out of his back in flashes of hard, rough white, a row of spikes from his neck to his rump. He screamed as his skull erupted in a mass of splinters and shivers and then he was rising, to bloody, long feet, tearing at the clothes on his back and roaring, a deep, guttural sound from within his belly that echoed down the alley.

He was on Freddie in seconds, a skinless monster with bony spines driven through his body, snarling and foaming at the gums, eyes wide and round and white. His teeth crashed down into Freddie's neck and he tore at the man's flesh, biting and scratching and howling, an animal. The thing plunged long, cracked fingers into Freddie's gut and tore out his liver and threw it aside, rummaging around in the cavern of the dark-skinned man's belly until it had driven its arm right up into Freddie's chest.

'Fuck,' Freddie croaked, and then the hand burst out of him, rupturing the cross carved into his skin in a mess of cracked ribs and torn-up lungs and blood. Freddie toppled, wet, onto the floor and the thing stood over him, bringing its bony fists down on the doctor's skull again and again and again until they just slopped around in all the wet, moaning and screaming and growling all the time.

Blood pooled around Freddie's face and seeped

into his open eyes, dark and unforgiving. With his palms flat on the concrete, his last prayer was answered, and he died before the beast could dig its teeth into his brain.

Skit clambered in through the open kitchen window at the back of the house and slid over the sink, careful not to bump his pockets on the edge of the basin for fear that he might shatter their contents. 'Hey!' he called, stumbling drunkenly over tiles clogged with crumbling plaster and shit. 'Any a you guys abou'?'

He reached up to turn the lights on, then remembered they had been shut off over a month ago. He toyed with the switch for a moment, high enough that the echoing *click-click-click* seemed almost like a rattling musical cue. Around him, the kitchen was a ruptured shell: the oven and the refrigerator had been taken out and in their place, great, black holes were stuffed with wires and chewed at the corners by rats; the cabinets had been stripped bare and the worktops removed so the whole room was a mismatched parlour of glue-painted, splintered surfaces and messy wooden frames. Skit passed into the hallway and dragged himself upstairs, calling out again halfway up.

'Hey, can one a youse put a torch on or sumth? Dark as *shit* in here.'

Above him, in one of the abandoned bedrooms, a white light crashed through the shadows and flickered.

He heard voices, low chatter in the dark.

'Much better,' he exclaimed, waving a hand dramatically. Skit was tall, lanky, with thin arms and legs, and he had to duck beneath a jutting outcrop of plaster as he reached the top of the stairs. His hair had grown to shoulder-length and began to curl around a scrawny neck criss-crossed with popping, pock-marked veins. His eyes were bright and rimmed with red and his nostrils almost met in the middle of his nose, separated only by a thin bridge of brittle, sore flesh. His chin was rough with beard and he wore a torn, leather jacket he'd found down by the old retail park, loose over a baggy jumper and skinny jeans that somehow fell about his narrow legs like flares. There was a hole in his left shoe, and the right was smeared with paint.

'Hey, Skitter,' Rowena murmured, glancing up at him from a week-old newspaper as he stepped into the bedroom. She liked the cartoons.

'Where's Reggie?' Skit said, glancing about the room. The bedframe had broken and sagged in the middle, but they didn't know where else to put it, so it stayed. In another corner, a battered double bed they'd dragged in from the skip down the street was stained with brown and yellow and black and puffy with hair. The floor was scattered with needles and points that had been casually kicked to the edges and glimmered in the light of the torch.

'Where you think?' Rowena said, nodding in the

direction of the piss-soaked mattress.

Skit hadn't seen Reggie at first. He was slumped over the mattress, thin and ragged, bare-chested with a ridged, bumpy spine shooting out of his back. So thin and hollow that he was almost invisible in the shadows.

'Hey, get yer head up, Reg,' Skit said, falling to his knees in front of the glowing torch. Light played off his pointed face and the shadow of his nose jabbed arrows of black into his eyeballs. Reggie hadn't moved. 'Come on, Reg, I got sumth you'll like. Both a you.'

Rowena grumbled. A strand of thin, red hair had fallen in her mouth and she blew it away. 'What is it, Skitter? If you found another painting in that skip we can't hang it, you threw that last one up on the only hook in the house.'

'Ah, but don't it look brilliant,' Skit whistled. 'Reg! Come on, up with you!'

Reggie groaned, rearing up from the shadows and crawling toward them on his hands and knees. 'What?' he growled. When he broke into the torchlight his face was lit in a flashing circle of white and his piercings glinted a faint, dancing grey. His lips were dusted with shining, silver paint.

'I got us something special,' Skit whispered.

'Has he found another fucking painting?' Reggie hissed.

'Don't think so,' Rowena said.

'Do you want to know, or what?' Skit said.

Reggie shrugged.

'So I'm walkin along, you know, minding my business, and come across this alley, right –'

'Just show us, you silly bollocks!' Rowena said.

'Fine,' Skit said, reaching into his coat. He spread them across the floor with delicate fingers, grinning into the torchlight. 'Look at this for a *haul.*'

'Is that…'

'Must be,' Skit said.

'Can't be,' Reggie said. 'Not pure. Skitter, that's a *lot.*'

Skitter stood up, almost kicking one of the things into the wall, and bowed elaborately.

Rowena leaned forward and picked one up, holding it into the light. The syringe seemed to glow with an ethereal white light and the fluid inside, thick and clear and dripping, flashed red.

'Who's up for a blast, then?' Skit said, crashing back to his knees and grabbing one of the syringes for himself.

Reggie grinned. 'This better be good shit, Skitter.'

'Oh, it is,' Skit said, nodding furiously. He looked into his own syringe and rolled up his trouser leg, pressing the tip of the needle to a spot just above his ankle. 'Trust me, this looks like the kind a shit that's gonna change your fuckin life.'

THE SHAPE OF DESPAIR

Jin heard yelling from downstairs, but it was muffled beneath the hoarse sounds of screaming and the buzz of a chainsaw in his ears.

He grunted, tapping *pause* on the keyboard and lifting the cushioned pad of one headphone off his ear. 'What?' he called, over the now-muted layers of shredded violin music that made up the game's title-screen soundtrack. The noise was tinny and faded and every second or two a burst of deep, electronically-enhanced double bass crashed through the little speakers held just above his eardrum.

'I said,' his mother shouted up the stairs, 'your dinner'll be ready in half an hour!'

'Fine!' Jin yelled, slapping the headphone back into place and turning to the screen. The monitor on his schoolwork-strewn desk was a grand's worth of high-definition plasma encased in a thin, white frame that seemed to hover over his keyboard, lit up in ever-shifting arcs of green and purple and red. Far too expensive a setup for a seventeen-year-old, Jin's mother had complained, but his father spoiled him just the same every Christmas since he ran off with the therapist that was supposed to be dealing more with his post-traumatic stress than the hard-boiled stress in his pants. Jin wished, sometimes, that his father had stuck around, but then he wouldn't have the computer or all the video games that had come pre-installed upon it, or the signed film cells from his favourite horror B-movies, or the wardrobe full of hoodies and expensive trainers.

Jin puffed air out of his cheeks, finger hovering over the mouse button. The screen screamed at him with blood-red font that looked as though it had been scratched out of the pixelated, black-and-white background: *Red Weeping: the game.* He was six-hours deep into the campaign and his wrists stung from being craned over the edge of the desk. His keyboard hand was sore. Quickly, he clicked off the game and opened up the library on his computer: a white-backed folder spiralled into view and he scrolled through his collection, leaning back lazily in a high-backed office chair that his mother had bought off the other Korean family down the world. She called the wife Small World Sally because every time they met she would say "another Asian household two doors down, small world!" and laugh. Jin didn't think her name was Sally.

'Better be finishing off up there!' his mother called up.

Jin nodded, not bothering to answer. He could smell tomato sauce and garlic wafting up through his closed bedroom door, lingering on the piles of clothes and the stacks of old, American horror novels crammed into one corner, over the posters and the jet-black carpet and his crumpled, two-week-old bedsheets. Something quick, he thought, quick and easy and just short enough to fill half an hour.

He scrolled through dozens of survival horror games and blood-spattered icons, sighing dramatically to himself. The scrolling stopped as the mouse came to hover on something he hadn't played yet, hadn't thought about playing yet. It had been free to download off the internet, and Jin usually liked to play the free ones so he could tell Jess how shit they were and they could laugh about it. He hadn't considered the game since.

It was called, *Shapes of Despair.*

He remembered the download page, a string of one and no-star reviews pasted beneath a stream of garbled text that marketed the thing as a "five-minute foray into the darkest corners of the soul". The reviews said it was nasty, that the creator was some sick piece of work and that it should be banned. Jin shrugged and opened the game.

The screen flickered black and a cluster of dead pixels flashed up in one corner. For a moment he caught a glimpse of his reflection; skinny, raven-black hair slicked purposefully in front of his eyes and melting into the black of the screen so that it looked as if the shallows had started to bite at the edges of his skull; glasses on the bridge of a thin nose and faint curls of ingrown moustache hair on his top lip. Then the black flickered white and gold and red and he winced at the brightness of the display, jamming it down frantically with his thumb.

The screen darkened again and the creator logo appeared: a pixelated rose crowned by a spiralling, purple-pink trail of thorns. *Babylon Flower Gaming,* said a line of white text beneath. Then the logo faded too and the black splintered in a spider's web of cracks that spread from the centre of the screen to the very edges and looked so realistic Jin had to squint to make sure the screen itself hadn't actually split.

The titles played. There was no music, no soundtrack at all. Blocky, colourful letters read *Shapes of Despair* (the spelling mistake was so obvious that Jin wondered how none of the creative team had picked it out before releasing the thing) and a subtitle in all black warned him *Beware – this game contains elements of survival horror that may not be suitable for younger players.* Below that, a single button. *Play.*

Jin hesitated, mouse hovering anxiously above the button. There was something about the colourful, almost playful tone of the title that made him uneasy, something about the splinters that still lingered on the screen and a background which was far too blurry to make out, a mess of brown and beige and deep, stained red. Shadows hung in the corners of the monitor and he glanced over his shoulder, compelled for some reason to make sure the door was still closed.

When Jin turned back to the screen the titles had disappeared. *Welcome to the game,* read a new line of text. He glanced down at his hand; his finger rested lightly on the mouse button. He must have clicked without realising, he thought. He must have.

The screen went black.

For a few moments there was silence, then the speakers clamped to his ears erupted with ragged, heavy breathing. Lights flickered and his character opened his eyes, shapes swimming as he seemed to stagger up from a surprisingly well-animated floor. The image settled and Jin squinted at the screen, tapping at the keyboard to figure out the controls. It looked like his character was in a kids' nursery, pastel-blue walls decorated with murals that showed cute little characters dancing under rainbows and clouds spraying shafts of colour into a starry sky. Rolling, green hills tumbled into the corners of the room. It looked good, he thought, graphics so realistic he could hardly make out the tell-tale softened corners and overly-vibrant colours that gave away the animation. When his character moved, he could hear the footfalls in his headphones.

He moved the character towards a cot in the corner

of the nursery, tramping loudly over plain, uncovered floorboards. The cot was empty, a white frame casting realistic shadows on a flattened nest of cushions and sheets draped with stars and moons. Jin swung his mouse around and the character looked all around the room: lights streamed in through a tall window and danced on the cracks between the floorboards; the ceiling was a swirled, gorgeous plane of plaster with a crescent-moon lampshade hanging from it and swinging a little.

Jin pushed his character to the door. Text flashed up at him: *Click to enter.* He clicked.

Locked, it said. He frowned. There had been nothing else to explore in the nursery, that he could see. Maybe he had missed something in the cot. A key, or some clue as to what he was supposed to do. He was eager to explore the rest of the house, found himself itching to get his character out of the nursery. The harsh breathing in his ears tightened.

Jin turned his character round and smiled when he saw it. Clever, he thought.

There was a toy, in the middle of the room, that hadn't been there before. Some mechanic in him trying to unlock the door had made it appear on the floorboards. He walked his man over to the thing and looked it over. The toy was something he'd seen a million times before, a wooden cube about the size of a shoebox with three designs cut out of its face: an opening in the shape of a square, lined with green; a similarly-lined circle, blue; a red-bordered triangle. He clicked, found that his player could pick up the toy and spin it around. He grinned, whirling the thing this way and that on-screen with the mouse, and then focused up and looked at the bottom.

The word *Objectives* was carved into the wood, followed by three lines of bloody text. The first had been crossed out, completed: ~~Find the box.~~

The second objective read, *Find the green cube.*

The third, *Find the blue cylinder.*

And finally, drizzling little trails of crimson onto the corners of the wooden toy, *Find the red prism.*

Jin frowned. 'That's it?' he murmured. The aim of the game was to complete the toy; to find the shapes and cram them into the box where they belonged. He couldn't see any survival horror elements to it, not in the brightly-lit nursery. Perhaps the horror began when he opened the door.

He clicked, dropping the toy soundlessly to the floorboards, where it drifted and rolled. He turned around and moved back to the door. *Click to open,* it said. He clicked.

The door opened on his bedroom. Jin froze as he saw, on the screen, pale walls lined with posters and signed film cells, stacks of pulp horror in one corner, crumpled clothes on the floor.

'No,' he whispered. 'It can't be…'

It couldn't. But it looked so much like his room, almost exactly the same. The only difference was the bed – there was something there, on the sheets, nestled among folds in the material and hidden almost completely away so that all he could see at first was a smudge of green. Jin leant closer to the screen, inspecting every detail. Slowly, he moved his character forward.

Game Complete, flashed a string of red font on the screen, and then it went black as the game shut itself down. Jin recoiled as a piercing, shrill whine came through the headphones and the computer rebooted itself in a flickering cluster of black and grey.

'What the fuck?' Jin said. He hadn't completed the game at all. He still had all three shapes to find – what the hell had just happened?

When the computer reloaded he tried to find the game again, but it was gone. He searched frantically, poring through his recently-uninstalled files, but there was nothing there, no trace of it at all. He searched for it online and found the download page, but the link had gone. He couldn't get it back.

'Dinner!' his mother yelled, and Jin jolted.

'Fuck,' he moaned, slumping back in his chair. His heart was pounding. There was a bug, or a glitch. The game was a broken piece of shit. 'Fuck this,' he murmured, tossing the headphones onto his desk and standing up.

There was something on his bed.

Jin froze again, skin crawling. He could hardly make it out – just a smudge of green nestled in the folds – but he knew what it was. Slowly, he moved to the bed and reached out to peel back the covers.

The green cube was the size of a fist, painted a lurid, neon shade and made of the same splintered wood as the toy in the game. The corners were rounded and, as he reached forward to pick it up, he found that it was oddly heavy. It sat in his palm, a green block from a kids' toy that he'd never owned and certainly never played with in this room, and yet it was right there, clutched in his shaking fingers.

It was real.

'What the fuck,' Jin repeated. The cube tumbled out of his hand onto the bed and he stumbled back from it, crashing into the office chair. It spun around and he lost his balance, grabbing the corner of his desk and looking down –

The toy was in his chair.

It sat, perfectly still, where he had been only seconds before. He had never seen it in his life, never except for in the wretched five minutes he had played that stupid, *broken* game and yet it was there, solid, the size of a shoebox: a hollow, wooden cube with three shapes carved out of its face.

Gingerly, he reached out and touched the thing. There was no bristle of electricity or crackle of static beneath his fingers, no poof of smoke or flashing knot of pixels – it was just *wood*. Slowly, carefully, he lifted the thing and cradled it in both arms. It was heavy, the wood must have been oak or mahogany or some shit, and he dropped it onto the bed, standing back to inspect it.

'Jin, it's getting cold!' his mother yelled.

'Coming!' he said. He stared at the box and his blood thinned with dread. A thought occurred to him, suddenly, and he pushed the box to topple it over. The bottom was carved with the same list of objectives he'd seen on-screen. The second, *Find the green cube,* had been crossed out, a thick, deep line scratched across it with a knife or a dreadful long claw.

Jin looked from the box to the green cube and swallowed. Slowly, he turned the box back over and reached for the little block. He paused – what the hell are you *doing,* he thought? – and then he jammed the little green cube into its slot in the face of the toy.

It wouldn't go in.

He frowned, pushing at the corners of the green block, trying to force it into the hole, but it wouldn't budge. He drew it out again and peered over the top of the box, looking in. Through the green-lined square he couldn't see all the way to the bottom of the box, just a deep, shadowy black.

Gripping the green cube in one hand, he slid the fingers of the other into the hole and felt around, screwing up his face in concentration. Rough, unsanded splinters of wood at the edge of the hole scraped against his knuckles and then, as he pushed his hand deeper inside, at his wrist. Maybe there was something in there already, he thought, stopping the block from going all the way in –

Jin howled as something grabbed his hand. He pulled his arm back but the thing had gripped his fingers and it squeezed, claws digging into his flesh. He gritted his teeth as a deep, stinging pain coursed up his wrist – pointed teeth pierced the soft skin between his thumb and index finger and he hissed in agony. The thing's grip loosened for a moment and he yanked upward; grey, clawed fingers thrust out of the square hole after him and scrabbled at his hand and he yelped, slamming the green cube down to crush the creature's knuckles against the wooden top of the toy.

'Get away from me!' Jin grunted, hammering again and again with the little green cube. Something inside the box rasped and he heard a crack, thrust the green cube down to push the claws back down into the dark. The cube settled, sliding into its slot in the box, and Jin staggered back from it, clutching at his bloody hand.

He breathed, ragged and heavy, panting with fear. He wiped at his hand with the hem of his shirt and saw the thing had left bitemarks in his skin, punctured it around his knuckles and dragged narrow strips of red along his fingers with its horrid, grey claws.

'What the *fuck,*' he breathed.

Someone knocked on the door and he cried out.

'Jin?' his mother called. 'What the hell's going on in there?'

She opened the door and her eyes dropped instantly to his bloody fingers.

'I just… caught my hand,' Jin lied, sliding it into his jeans pocket. 'Sorry, I'm coming now.'

'Are you okay?' his mother said. Her gaze fell on the box. 'What's that?'

'I don't know,' Jin said, and he stepped past her out of the room, hardly daring to look back.

'You find that in an old toybox or something?'

Jin turned, reaching past her to draw his door closed. 'Something,' he said, and he followed her downstairs for dinner.

He ate in silence a hollow pit curling at the base of his gut. Usually he would eat pizza with his fingers but he cut it with a knife and fork, acting on some automatic, low-level instinct and moving as slowly as he could in some meandering attempt to put off the inevitable. He didn't want to go back up there. It was waiting for him, on the bed, the box. He had cleaned up his hand; it wasn't so bad, once all the blood had washed away, but he'd still had to use half a packet of plasters to cover all the scratches and pock-marks on his skin. His little finger ached and sent dull, shooting pains into his wrist whenever he pressed too hard with his knife; he thought the grey-skinned demon in the box might have sprained it.

'Everything okay, Jinny?' his mother said. She had almost finished. She sat at the other end of the table, red sauce dripping from the tips of long, lacquered fingernails. Hyun-ae was still dressed in her work clothes, a pale, peach-coloured shirt with a black-lined collar and a pale grey skirt; the jacket was draped over the back of her chair.

'Everything's fine,' he said, keeping his eyes down. The thing's skin had felt so cold and rough and wrinkled, wet enough to leave his hand cool and sticky, even after he had jammed it back into the wretched box. He could feel it, now, gripping his wrist in a deathly, tight-fingered embrace, and he wished he'd never opened the game – it was ridiculous, it couldn't be real. He had imagined the whole thing.

He was insane.

'Did I tell you the Morrisons put an offer in for that house on Herbert Street?' she said, tearing a slice off her plate and shredding at the corner with her teeth. Red flecks of tomato danced about her gums as she spoke. 'Came all the way across from America after some tragedy, said their daughter had gone away somewhere – can't remember where, though, for the life of me, she was a navy captain or a boatswain or something like that – said the little place was just what they were looking for. Did I tell you about that, Jin?'

'No, mother,' Jin said, smiling thinly across the table. He raised his fork and poked a scrap of wet, dripping dough between his lips. He chewed slowly, thoughts on the heavy green cube and the splintered wooden toy and the stupid *game* –

'Are you listening to me, Jinny?'

He raised his head, lifting his eyebrows. 'Sorry, what?'

'Oh, you are *just* like your father,' Hyun-ae scolded. She stood from the table, nodding at his plate. 'You finish that, Jin, I'll go see what we've got in the freezer for dessert.'

'Alright,' Jin mumbled.

She drew her plate off the table and swept out of the room and Jin was alone, chewing silently as he worked the knife through another slice. Serrated metal squealed on ceramic as the blade dragged over his plate. Absent-mindedly, he tossed another shred of pizza into his teeth and bit down.

Something cracked.

Jin swore, raising a hand to his mouth. His gums froze, millimetres apart, and he winced as warmth spread over his tongue. He glanced down at the plate, wondering if he'd bit down on something solid. Slowly, he reached into his mouth and pulled out the half-chewed clump of red nestled in his cheek, smearing it on the side of his plate.

Cautiously, he poked at his stinging tooth with the tip of his finger. A sharp shock of pain seared the side of his face and he reeled, retracting his hand and staring. There was blood, a thin, wet bead of it mixed with saliva and spit. His eyes widened and he reached in again, feeling around for whatever had broken.

Jin found the cracked tooth and balked as he pulled, twisting it inadvertently. It had split right down the middle, a severed molar right near the back of his jaw, and the two fractured pieces wiggled independently as he prodded at them. The roots of the tooth seemed to swirl and carve a stinging, jarring circle out of his gum and as he drew his finger back again, he found the thing that he had bitten down on, the solid, rough thing that was nestled now in the soft flesh of his gum, and he pulled.

The splinter came out with a soft spray of blood that trickled out of his pierced gum and onto his tongue and he spat it onto the table, hacking and moaning and clamping a hand over his mouth as the pain bled through to the back of his throat.

'Jinny?' his mother called from the freezer. 'You okay in there, love?'

He didn't answer. His eyes were locked on the thing on the table, covered in his blood and decorated with a tiny speck of white, a fragment of his broken tooth: it was a long, pointed splinter of blue wood. Almost the length of his sprained little finger and the width of a fork prong, it glistened with beads of red but the paint along its rough shaft was the same pleasant, pastel-blue he had seen on the walls of the nursery, the same that had been painted around the edge of the second hole in the box's wooden face.

Find the blue cylinder.

Jin shook his head, lurching out of his chair. 'This isn't real,' he moaned. 'This isn't fucking real.' He turned, shooting out of the dining room as another digging pain cracked at the inside of his top lip. He reached the bathroom and staggered in, slamming the door shut behind him and bolting it, doubled over at the sink as he reached into his mouth.

He watched his reflection in the mirror as shaking fingers dug between his front teeth and slowly, carefully, slid out another splinter. It was the same awful blue and almost as long and the point was split, forked like a snake-tongue into two sharp, blood-dotted spines. He tossed it into the sink and gagged as something flitted over his tonsils. Mouth open wide, he ran the sink and leant over and spat into the bowl. Flecks of wood sprayed out from between his teeth in a mess of saliva and blood and harsh, splintered blue and they swirled toward the drain. He gargled, streams of mucus pouring from his lips, reaching in with his thumbs to claw at the shivers of wood digging at his cheeks and gums and tongue, pawing them out wildly and letting them fall, streaked with red, into the basin.

'Jin! What's going on in there?'

He couldn't answer. He tried to talk but the only sound that came out of his mouth was a hoarse, jarring *ack-aack* and now there was something buried in his throat, something impossibly wide and suffocating. He couldn't breathe. His eyes bulged and he grabbed at his neck, scraping the skin with his nails. Oh, it *hurt*. He wrapped a hand around the lump in his throat and squeezed, almost trying to push it up into his mouth – he could feel it, beneath layers of skin, round and solid and splintered, scratching and peeling at the inside of his throat, and black spots danced before his eyes as he drew in a ragged breath and let out a gasping, gurgling whisper.

His tongue was bleeding. He pressed two fingers into his mouth and ribbons of fleshy, wet muscle flapped against them, spraying blood over his hand and the sink. He wanted to sob with the pain but his eyes were peeled open and bone dry and he couldn't blink, couldn't see out of them. The pads of his fingers brushed splintered tonsils and he heaved, but the thing in his throat blocked all the bile and vomit from rising into his mouth and it sank back down in a putrid wave of stinging, vile fluid. His lungs strained and he tried to retch again, to force the thing upward; it was solid and stuck and all he could do was choke on it.

Outside, the hammering on the bathroom door stopped.

'Muh…' Jin gasped. Then the thing in his neck was pushing itself, thrusting up toward the base of his skull and pressing against the back of his tongue, pinning it down. He heard a *crack!,* couldn't tell if it was the thing or his jawbone but it didn't matter, all that mattered was opening his mouth wide enough that the thing could push out through his teeth. He screamed, the shrill noise barely a whisper as his teeth crashed and splintered outwards and the thing forced his jawbone down, down, down –

Crack!

There it was again and this time he knew it was his skull, knew that the connection between his jaws had ruptured and it was hanging off his face, streaming with blood, and still the thing pushed as his head tipped forward, smacking the edge of the sink. Black hair cut his vision into dark strands and he spluttered as finally, painfully, the thing crashed out through his shredded lips and fell to the tiled floor with a *knok* and bounced.

Jin collapsed, crashing to his knees, raising both shaking hands to his jaw but afraid to touch it, face frozen in a moaning, gasping scream. His mouth was fractured and petrified in the round, thick shape of the thing that had burst out of his throat and he blinked rapidly, tears finally streaming from his burning eyes.

The blue cylinder rolled over the floor and laid itself to rest against the pillar of the sink. Strings of mucus and blood run through with flecks of torn cartilage dragged up from his oesophagus swung from his lips as he flung himself towards the door, lunging at the bolt and opening it and moaning wordlessly.

The door opened and he howled.

Hyun-ae was spread across the floor, clothes torn from her, naked body ripped apart and strewn over the carpet in a mess of blood and spiralling organs. Stringy torrents of meat as red as the tomato sauce on the pizza burst outward in a sloppy, almost-liquefied explosion of wet, warm death and in the middle of it all, cradled in her cracked ribcage, was the box.

'Nuh...' Jin moaned. His broken jawbone rattled and shots of agony crashed through his skull as he shook his head. 'Hhahhh...'

The box tipped towards him, barrelling over pointed ribs and crushing them as it rolled and crashed against the doorframe. He caught a glimpse of the bottom:

~~Find the blue cylinder.~~

'Huhhh...' he sobbed. He could hardly move his head but he rolled his eyes down and saw it, in the corner of his vision, the pastel-blue block slick with blood and dotted with tiny, brittle chunks of his teeth. I don't want to, he thought. I can't...

Something growled from inside the box.

Jin wailed, scrambling back to the sink. His hand bumped the cylinder and he shuddered, eyes locked on the toy as shadows moved and twisted behind the two empty slots in its face. He caught a flash of grey, spiny teeth and he whimpered.

Why are you doing this to me? he thought. What came out was, 'Hhuuhhh…'

For a moment everything was still. There was no sound, save for the crashing of his heart and the steady drip of blood on the tiles. And then, piercing, a whisper from inside the box.

Spindly grey arms thrust out of the holes and twisted themselves around the box; two of them, at first, then a third and a fourth and a fifth until the toy was crowned by a sprawling mess of bony limbs that clutched at the doorframe and yanked it forward; it tumbled onto its face and dozens of scuttling claws *clack*ed on the tiles as it walked across to him and then it flipped, and the arms thrashed at his face, swiping with grey-skinned ferocity before writhing and disappearing back into the shadows of the box.

The demon looked up at him through the blue-lined, circular slot and it grinned. Its eyes were white and bloodshot and tiny, sunk deep into the dark inside the toy. It hissed and a grey tongue flitted between murky teeth.

Shaking, Jin reached for the blue cylinder and wrapped his fingers around its crest, lifting it off the floor. You want this? he thought, and he said, 'Yuuh… wuhhh…'

Have it, he thought. 'Haahh…'

Jin thrust the blue cylinder forward, reluctant to put

his hands anywhere near the snapping claws of the thing in the box. It grabbed the block from his hands and a loud *shuk* echoed about the bathroom as it slid into place.

The demon-creature whistled gleefully and the box tipped back so that Jin could see the bottom again. The third objective was still there, hadn't been struck through.

Find the red prism.

Jin shook his head. Tears streamed down his face and his hand moved to his belly. What the hell kind of sick game was this? It was all a nightmare, some bloody, brutal nightmare he couldn't blink out of. His head lolled back and his gaze shifted to his mother's face, burst apart in a messy spatter of brain and bone and split eyeballs. Her hair was flung about the room and draped over the walls in knots and blood-matted curls of black.

The box flipped over again and spiny, grey arms poked out of the triangular slot, scratching at the crimson edges in some withered kind of desperation.

'Nuuh,' he moaned. No. I won't do it…

The box lay still. Quiet. Jin could feel himself fading out of consciousness but something kept him awake, a rush of adrenaline that almost hurt, a terrified sense of fight-or-flight that left him hollow and wrecked but entirely awake, more alert than he had ever been. He could hear the splintering above his head but he didn't want to look.

A single, shadowy arm poked out of the box and pointed upward.

Slowly, Jin stood up, leaning heavily on the edge of the sink. His legs wanted to give way but he held himself there, weak and tortured and certain that he needed an ambulance and oh *god,* his mother was dead —

The mirror was cracked.

Not just cracked but splintered; the mirror above the bathroom sink was cracked from its centre to its very edges, and he knew at once that it was the same pattern of spider-web crevices that had appeared on his computer screen before the game opened. Written on the fractured glass, smeared with red ink that dripped with tiny, stuck hairs and flecks of skin and a single, lacquered fingernail, were the words:

Click to open.

Jin looked down. The box stood by his feet, and through the red triangle he saw the demon's eyes glint with hunger. He shook his head.

The arm thrust out of the box again and a single, clawed finger bent upwards: *Like this,* it seemed to say. Then the narrow fingers curled into a fist and it made a thrashing, punching motion.

Jin turned his eyes back to the mirror.

Slowly, he raised a hand, his good hand, and he clenched his knuckles into a tight, trembling fist, mirroring the little horrid grey thing's movements. He

243

didn't have a choice, he supposed. The box had appeared in his room of its own accord, the cylinder block in his throat without warning. It was impossible, all of it. There was no such thing as a game that broke out of the computer and killed your mother.

But he knew if he didn't open the mirror, it would open itself.

He pulled back his fist and launched it forward, moaning as pain crashed across his knuckles. It didn't break all at once but the splintered surface grew frost with hair-thin openings and he punched it again, sobbing and streaming and bleeding onto his clothes, and again, and again, until the mirror shattered – not outwards, with all the shards tumbling onto the floor in an iridescent shower of flat, jagged pieces, but in, as if there were some secret compartment behind the mirror that they had all fallen into.

Through the empty frame, Jin saw death. It flickered, once, the corners all pixelated and shining, and then the air seemed to thicken with a shimmering heat haze and it was real, real and stinking – sulphur and blood and smoke and *shit* and his mother's ruptured insides.

Pillars of flame rose up from geysers and crevices torn out of a barren, black-ash wasteland. The sky through the mirror was a burning, bright red and the sun hung in chopped-up, white slices from a ring of orange clouds, swinging like a pendulum in long, slow arcs across the chaotic mess of the world behind Jin's bathroom wall.

The red prism, a triangular wooden block painted so dark that he could hardly see it through all the fire, sat in the sand, untouched by the swirling dust and the twisting, black shadows that coursed over the salt planes. It all seemed to go on for miles. Great, white worms lurched up from the sand and crashed back down, hissing and shrieking all the while. Blood rained from harsh, spitting mouths crammed with pointed teeth set into the trunks of burnt, blackened trees, branches curling outward like claws. Little grey beasts roamed over the sand and swiped at each other, grunting and snarling and laughing, giggling like children.

Find the red prism.

With one last, terrified look at the box, Jin reached over the sink and thrust his hand through the mirror.

THE NOTE
AN EPILOGUE

It's not enough. Not alone.

You'd think it would be enough, because it's fucking awful.

It's a shitstorm of late-night sobbing until you throw up all your guts in the sheets and sometimes it lays on top of you so heavy you'll piss yourself right there in the mattress and just lay in it unless you can sum up the strength to roll off onto the floor. And when you get down there, all curled up in a ball pushing tears out your eyes and still pissing with a little bit of vomit still on your tongue, you think, *it couldn't get any worse than this,* and it does.

It's a plague of despair and sometimes it's not even despair, or sadness, or any feeling at all. It's the opposite – just a thick, dark blanket of nothing that pulls itself round you so tight you can't lift your arms or your head and you wonder what the living fuck you ever did to deserve this.

I know what I did.

It's different every day. Sometimes it's not there at all, and on those days you think *how could the world ever be so fucking dark* and then the darkness comes, the next day, and maybe it hangs around for a few hours or a few days or it's on-and-off for a year, but it comes, and it goes when *it* wants to go, not when *you* want it to, and all that time you think *yeah. Oh yeah,* that's *how.* Sometimes it's just a flash, just a tiny blink-and-you'll-be-glad-you-missed-it moment in the corner of a second but it hurts just as bad as if it clung to you for a week.

It's pain and guilt and whatever the word is sorrow, sorrow so harsh and so deep you'll wish you were dead, but you won't have the strength to end it.

It's not enough for *that.*

It never has been for me, anyway. There was a moment, back when I was finishing high school and my girlfriend pushed my head down into the water in the kitchen sink at her parents' house and told me she wouldn't take her hand off my scalp till I said I'd change. I didn't know what I was supposed to change, but it didn't happen, clearly, because she stamped on my foot in her Doc Martens a week later and broke three of my toes. The moment came, and I thought, *I could.* But I didn't. It wasn't enough.

It was enough for Tim Kelton. I remember reading about him in some article written by a choked-up university student who I think was on a shit-tonne of heroin and halfway through a law degree she hadn't read for. She said Kelton had nearly done it a few times, and she'd talked him down from a couple. Then this

251

time came, the last time, and finally – *finally!* – it was enough for Tim Kelton, and they found him a day later with his legs dangling over a stool and his neck all bent up. They say the stool leg cracked before he could kick it away.

I don't know what they'll say about me.

I don't know how they'll ~~you'll~~ find me, either. I'll leave this somewhere obvious, so you won't have to look too hard. I won't make it messy, if I can help it. But I haven't thought about how I'm going to do it yet. The internet says a bullet is the quickest way, but the only gun I've ever seen is the air rifle my uncle keeps locked up in his garage and brings out on Sundays to shoot rats in his garden, and I don't know if the pellet from that would go more than an inch into my skull. I know I wouldn't be able to bring myself to jump. I want it to be peaceful.

Maybe after what I've done, I don't deserve peaceful.

However you find me, know that I'm sorry, and know that it wasn't the depression. That wouldn't ever have been enough. It might have tempted me a couple of times – who knows, maybe in a few years it would have proved me wrong. But that's not why I'm hanging here now.

Maybe I have decided how I'll do it. Maybe Tim Kelton had the right idea.

It wasn't the depression, whatever it looks like from the outside. It was *him.* Not Kelton.

The Devil.

He got to the others too. Christ, even Lawrence phoned me the other night to say he'd seen him. In a dream, he said. I told him to fuck off. Two nights later, I saw him. In a dream. ~~You'll read this and think I'm fucking insane~~ Please, believe me. This isn't some drug-fuelled fuck-rant, this is true. Maybe it was just a dream, but he *knew.*

He knew what we did to her.

She was only a kid.

We were all kids. Sure, we were older than her, but we didn't know what we were doing. I bet that's what they all say, right? But it's true. We were just playing around. We never thought about it. It just *happened.*

The dream felt real enough to *be* real but it couldn't have been, because he was impossible. A part of me doesn't want to tell you what he looked like, because you won't believe a word of it, but I have to.

He had a skull for a head.

Not a human skull, a deer skull, or a yak or some shit. And he was wearing a suit – a bright, white suit like a gangster. Black shoes, though, with these little pointy tips. And he said, *it's time to pay me back,* like I'd taken something from him. And then he walked me to the edge of the road and put his hand on the back of my head like he was about to push my head underwater, but I couldn't wake up. All I could do was look as he tipped my head over the edge of the road and showed me. Like I needed to be reminded.

Her back was all shredded where we dragged it over the tarmac. She was still alive, and we were standing over her like we were somehow surprised that we'd nearly killed her. And then Lawrence grabbed a rock and held it over her head and I stopped him – not the me that was watching, now, but the old me, the young me, the me that drove the car she was chained too. And I said, *what the fuck are you doing,* and he said, *she's not going to make it, we can't just leave her,* and I said, *we have to leave her.*

We watched for twenty minutes while she twitched and sobbed and died.

Then the man with the antlers pulled me back and said, *kill yourself.*

That was it. That was all he said. I woke up, and the next night I had the same dream, except this time he had taken his skull off and the head underneath was made of roadkill.

He said, *kill yourself.*

When you find me, make sure you get to Lawrence. If he hasn't done the same already, make sure he doesn't. He was the only one of us decent enough to try and put that girl out of her misery, and I was the shitfuck that stopped him. I deserve this.

I'm going to sleep one more night, and if he comes again and says, *kill yourself,* I'll get out of bed and do it. It'll be spontaneous. I'll figure it all out then. And if he doesn't come, if I don't dream of the man in the white suit and the skull, then I'll burn this note and find another way to deal with the guilt.

It's not enough, but he is.

ORIGINS

THE RAGE

The idea for this began as a simple thought that it would be a nice twist to pull off. Along the way, I changed the setting from a big, glowing sci-fi lab to an abandoned hospital ward and abandoned pretty much initial idea I had. So if anyone asks: yes, it went exactly as planned.

CARRION GODS

This was originally called "The Walker" and it was one of the first short stories I ever wrote. The first draft was about six times longer but got cut way down as soon as I realised there's only so much horror you can cram into a single stretch of road. The original version preached the whole "don't treat nature like shit" thing a bit more strongly. I'm not a huge one for preaching. That said, don't treat nature like shit.

GLIMMERMAN

This one came from a longer piece; in a novel I've been working on for about six months, there's a horrible, yellow-faced character with the nickname "Glimmerman"; in the book, there's a reason for that which stems from some folk tale about mining, but here I wanted to take the name itself and work from it to create something new – the nickname comes, in reality, from a weirdly interesting piece of Irish history that's definitely worth looking up. They weren't all like Connor Corbett.

THE POSSESSION OF MATHESON KEMBLE

Kemble is a character I've used a couple of times before, but only in passing, and I wanted to give him a stab at being more the focus of the piece. I also hated him from the moment I thought him up – could you tell?

SKIN

This was meant to be a full-blown cult story but I stumbled on something that I thought was a little more interesting. It's also the only story in this collection written in present tense, something I don't tend to play with an awful lot. And don't worry – there's plans to get to the bottom of what *really* happened to the Tracey Twins in my second collection.

LAIR OF THE LEECH (SHUDDERING DE'ATH: PART ONE)

I always wanted to include a vampire story in this collection, and I had some vague idea in my head about the owner of a creepy, Innsmouth-type aquarium. Throw in the image of an abandoned retail park (something quite easy to imagine at the time this was written) and it all came together.

WENDIGO WEEPING (SHUDDERING DE'ATH: PART TWO)

As soon as the idea for a short-story collection of any kind came into being, I knew that I had to throw in a two-parter. Of course it wouldn't end up being the only one (see below) but in those first days of planning the whole thing the idea of some kind of cliffhanger ending leading into another, slightly-different story seemed like something I thought could work.

LEVIATHAN SONG

A vague attempt at something like Lovecraftian, otherworldly horror was always going to be difficult, but this ended up being the hardest piece in the book to write purely because of the number of characters and the weird, unfamiliar setting (to me, at least) of a submarine. I'll admit it was nice to cram a time-travel twist into this book somehow, and even if this was a little predictable hopefully it was still fun.

X238 (THE RAGE: PART TWO)

Well, it had to happen, didn't it?

THE SHAPE OF DESPAIR

Perhaps the most experimental piece in the book, I was never sure about this one until I realised I didn't have to be. Weirdly, what happened to Jin ended up being one of the least bleak outcomes in the book, so perhaps this one was a nice story to go out on. I couldn't put into words where the idea of mixing my own nightmare version of Hell with that simple, match-the-shapes children's toy came from (didn't we all have those?), but here's hoping the ones you let your kids play with aren't manufactured by Babylon Flower. Oh, and we're not done with them, either.

Well, you made it. Thanks to everyone who encouraged the writing of this complete abomination of a book, and to everyone who's taken even a cursory glance at it since.

Here's to my second collection, **TALES FROM THE CAMBIUM HEART**, coming sometime... yeah, sometime. That sounds about right.

Printed in Great Britain
by Amazon